ONCE UPON A SEXY SCROOGE

ELLA FRANK

BROOKE BLAINE

SYNOPSIS

Ah, Christmas. The most magical time of the year. A time when the snow is falling, cider is flowing, and couples are kissing under the mistletoe.

Too bad all that makes me want to gag.

Look, it isn't that I'm a hater, it's just that I have a job to do, and this particular holiday is getting in the way of that. And I know what you'll say, that Micah Noble's Christmas Tree Farm is a beloved tradition for many of the families of Merrihill, but you have to see the bigger picture here: a five-star luxury resort where overworked Manhattanites can escape to, a serene place of spas and shopping and watching sexy lumberjacks chopping wood...

Oh, wait, scratch that last one. Lumberjacks aren't my thing. Anymore. Micah Noble cured me of that, which tends to happen when you're trying to buy someone's family land to bulldoze to the ground.

He can call me a Scrooge all he wants, but business is business, and pleasure is...well, not something I can afford to think about. Even if it does come packaged in those tight jeans and flannel shirts that make me want to rip them off with my teeth—

No. This is not happening. I will not think of Micah as anything other than an obstacle to getting what I want. A really, really sexy obstacle.

Ugh. Screw Christmas and the sleigh it rode in on.

MAXWELL

Present Day

$\mathcal{A}$S I SAT in my car in the never-ending traffic jam that was Midtown Manhattan, I scowled at each and every one of the pedestrians who strolled so happily down the sidewalks with their heaps of shopping bags, their bright eyes taking in the overdone holiday window displays like they'd never seen an animatronic Santa before.

The whole scene made me roll my eyes.

Didn't they know there was nothing magical about this time of year? Thousands of people piled into the city, cramming our already strained subways and streets, pouring money into big-box stores that only cared about their bottom dollar and how to win the rat race.

I would know. I was one of them.

With the traffic still unmoving, I put my car in park and sighed, letting my head drop against the headrest.

Was it just me, or had this year been a constant struggle to keep my head above water? It didn't make sense, though. I'd moved up in the company I worked for, an acquisitions firm at the top of its game, so finances would never be a worry. I had more money than I knew what to do with, not that it helped much in my current circumstances, other than the heated seats keeping my ass warm.

Horns blasted all around me, and I looked up to see the light had flipped to green, but the mass of people on the crosswalk hadn't eased. It was a damn free-for-all, and some of the taxi drivers had apparently had enough.

They inched forward, almost close enough to graze, but that didn't do much to give them a clear path. But once a pair of men stepped onto the crosswalk carrying a Christmas tree between them, the shouts began.

"Get outta the damn road!"

"Hey! You want a pair of broken legs for Christmas?"

"Imma shove that tree right up your—"

Aaand on that note, I hit the button to close the inch of window I'd had down for some fresh air.

Christmas. It brought out the best in everyone.

I glanced at my watch and tapped on the steering wheel, my patience running thin. I'd been due at the office nearly fifteen minutes ago, but thanks to this circus, I was now running late. Didn't these people have places to be? Families to visit or something? Surely after five department stores, they all started to look the same.

But as people hurried across the street weaving in and

out of the idling vehicles, it was starting to look like they had the better idea. Maybe I should get out and walk the last five blocks. It would probably be quicker.

As the light cycled back to red without us moving an inch, I turned on the radio and groaned at the DJ wishing everyone a merry Christmas. See, this was the problem with this particular holiday—you couldn't escape it. The second that last bite of turkey was eaten, it was as though a switch was flipped and everything turned sparkly and new.

There was even a set playlist for this time of year that was pulled out and played ad nauseum until everyone was so sick of the songs they were happy when they were put away for the other eleven months of the year.

It was a farce, the whole damn thing. A scheme dreamed up by greedy men who decided it was just another way to make a buck.

"So cynical, Max. What happened to make you that way?"

I blinked as the deep, familiar voice filled my head. It was so clear that I even caught myself looking at my empty passenger seat as a sappy song about coming home for Christmas started to play on the radio.

Seriously, now I was hallucinating?

I squeezed the bridge of my nose and shut my eyes, my mind wandering back to a small town outside of the city. A place where, for a moment in time, I'd forgotten the hustle and bustle of the real world and been swept up by holiday magic...

MAXWELL

One Year Earlier

"**Y**OU THINK YOU can pull this deal off and be back in the city by Christmas?"

My jaw twitched as I resisted the urge to tell my colleague at Willett-Goss to mind his business. "Doubting me, Patrick?"

"No, but it's a tough turnaround, even for you, and the holidays make people more sentimental about holding on to shit."

"Well, Micah Noble hasn't met me. He doesn't know just how persuasive I can be when there's something I want."

Patrick laughed down the phone. "Isn't that the damn truth."

I ignored the voice in the back of my mind that tried to

remind me I'd already been shut down by the Noble family several times over the phone, but that was exactly why I'd decided to drive to Vermont only days before Christmas. In the decade I'd worked in acquisitions, I hadn't lost a property yet, and I sure as hell wasn't about to start now that a promotion to partner was dangling over my head.

A sign on the side of the road announcing *Noble's Christmas Tree Farm, five miles* caught my attention as I carefully navigated an icy curve.

"Patrick, I'm almost there. I'll let you know when the deal is done." Then I ended the call just as the tires of my Lexus decided to slide over the yellow line into the other lane. A car coming from the opposite direction flashed its lights at me as it drew closer, and I instinctively jerked the wheel to the right.

"Shit." I lost control and tried to right myself, holding my breath as I braced for impact. But a few seconds later the other car passed without incident, and I let out a long sigh.

Driving up here felt like I was on a damn Slip 'N Slide, and I was over it.

"Haven't they ever heard of salt?" I muttered, slowing down.

Why anyone would choose to live somewhere that got snow up to their roof was beyond me. It was bad enough navigating the city when that stuff fell, but out here? One wrong move and you could end up sliding into a snowdrift on the side of the road, never to be seen again.

That wasn't how I planned to go.

I loosened my grip on the steering wheel and stared at the fat snowflakes hitting my windshield. They were coming much faster now, and if I didn't want to get stranded out here, I needed to move.

I slowly pressed my foot on the gas and began to inch the car forward, gingerly navigating the road and turning what should've been a ten-minute drive into twenty. But when I spotted a large wooden gate shoved open with *Noble's Christmas Tree Farm* on a sign hanging above it, I let out a sigh of relief.

I'd made it—and in one piece, too. It was a Christmas miracle.

I looked at the winding road that led into the property, and spotted a log cabin a little ways up the plowed path. There was smoke curling up out of one of the chimneys, and off in the distance a barn that towered up behind the cabin.

It was exactly what you'd imagine if someone said "think of a log cabin in the woods," and wouldn't you know, there was even a man out the front of it chopping wood.

Well, I wasn't going to get any deals done sitting out in my car like some sort of creeper. It was time to put my money where my mouth was. I turned into the property and, as I drove up toward the cabin, took a second to look around.

Out to my left, as far as the eye could see, were rows and rows of pine trees. Some big and some small, but all of them were capped and dusted with the snow falling, making the place look like a winter wonderland.

It was beautiful, picturesque even. I could see why someone wouldn't want to give it up. But I could *also* see the potential for others to enjoy it... Say, in a luxury resort.

Not that you'd find *me* staying in the middle of

nowhere, but there was an overwhelming interest for those wanting to escape the city on weekends and to anywhere other than the Hamptons.

I stopped a few feet away from the lumberjack guy—hey, maybe he'd come in handy when we had to clear the lot—and shut off the engine. As I stepped out of my car, I buttoned my suit jacket and looked up at the cabin. It was a quaint little version of what we planned to build, albeit on a much more extravagant scale. Yes, this was the perfect spot, though we'd have to make sure the roads coming up this way got some work.

"You lost?"

It took me a minute to realize the voice had come from the guy chopping wood, and as I glanced over to where he stood, I did a double take.

Taller and more built than I'd originally thought, he had to be at least six-five, but that wasn't the only thing that stood out about him.

The man was undeniably the most ruggedly sexy human I'd ever seen. I had never been hot for a guy with a beard before, but this man was changing my opinion on that quick fucking fast. It was thick and brown but kept short, and matched his hair that was buzzed on one side while leaving the rest swooped over in a devil-may-care style that fell into his eyes.

He brushed the hair back with his forearm, and the red and black flannel shirt he wore tightened against his broad chest.

And don't even get me started on the jeans that fit his narrow waist and muscled thighs like a glove—

"You're a day early. The tree farm doesn't open until tomorrow, so you'll have to come back then."

I snapped myself out of my perusal. If he thought dressed like I was, in the car I drove, that I was here for a tree then he was denser than I expected from someone so small town.

Instead of responding and wasting my breath—and also because it was cold as shit and I needed to warm up ASAP—I headed toward the stairs of the cabin. But as I rounded the front of my car, my dress shoes slipped on a patch of ice and I began to fall. I grabbed on to the hood of my car just as a strong hand reached for my arm to hold me up.

Humiliated, I righted myself and jerked my arm free. "I'm fine. I've got it."

Lumberjack snorted. "Yeah, that's obvious."

I dusted my hands off on my jacket, the snow from the hood turning them icy cold, as I turned on my judgmental savior and did my best to regain some semblance of control.

"I just have to get my bearings, that's all."

Lumberjack eyed me up and down and, as he turned away, muttered, "You're gonna need a lot more than that."

What the hell did that mean?

Incensed by the obvious insult, and the fact that this man somehow found *me* lacking, I stormed after him. Not the easiest thing to do when the ground was practically a skating rink and snow continued to fall in my eyes.

"Look, I don't know how things are run around here, but I didn't come out here to be insulted."

Lumberjack stopped by his pile of wood and picked up the ax leaning against it. "Who said I was insulting you?"

"I did, and I don't think your boss would like that very much."

"Hmm...*or* maybe he'd think you were rude and unthankful and do exactly the same thing."

Okay, I was done dealing with this guy. "You know what, I don't have time for this. If you could point me in the direction of Mr. Noble, we'll just forget this ever happened."

Lumberjack picked up the ax, resting the head against one of his mammoth shoulders, and took a step forward. Then, to my utter shock and dismay, held his other hand out.

"Micah Noble, and let me guess, you're Maxwell Scott."

MICAH

*W*ELL *WOULD YOU look at that,* I thought as Maxwell's jaw all but hit the icy ground he'd just slipped on. *The king has finally deigned to step out of his kingdom for five seconds of his life.*

I wasn't usually the spiteful type, but I couldn't help but take some kind of pleasure in just how out of place he seemed standing there in his designer shoes and perfectly tailored suit. Talk about a fish out of water. He looked as though he was dressed for a board meeting, not trekking it out here to snow country. But hey, if he wanted to get hypothermia, who was I to stop him?

"*You're* Micah Noble?" The look on Maxwell's face was comical. I was obviously the last person he'd expected to find when he pulled up, and considering I was outside doing what he'd no doubt consider a menial task, I hardly expected him to correlate me with the owner of this property.

"No, I'm Santa Claus. This is just my disguise."

Maxwell arched a brow as his eyes shifted to my outstretched hand, and when it was clear he wasn't going to take it, I shook my head.

"Look, why don't I save you some time, effort, and a pair of expensive leather shoes? What you're selling, I'm not interested in buying. So why don't you slip and slide your way back to the car and drive on out of here."

I turned back to my pile of wood and grabbed one of the stumps to place it on the wooden block.

"Mr. Noble."

My lips curled at the much *politer* tone as I balanced the wooden stump and turned back to face the man I'd started to refer to as Scrooge in my head. He was straightening his lapels and looked as though he was gearing up to feed me some line about how rich he could make me if I just signed on the dotted line. But money wasn't a factor for me, and unfortunately for him, that was all he had to offer.

"You still here?" I leaned the ax up against the side of the house and crossed my arms.

"Yes, I, well... I think we got off on the wrong foot."

"You think?" I lowered my eyes down his tailored pant legs and shrugged. "Maybe you should just count your lucky stars you're still *on* your feet."

Maxwell bristled at the jab, twin spots of color heating his cheeks, and I couldn't help but think how adorable he looked even as I wished him the hell off my property.

"Okay, fine. Was I a bit of an ass? Sure. But I've had a long drive, I obviously underestimated the weather, and I'd like nothing better than to go inside somewhere that isn't forty below to discuss why I'm here."

"I know why you're here. And I'll say it again: I'm not interested."

"You haven't even heard me out."

"And I don't plan to." I took a step toward Maxwell and straightened my shoulders. He wasn't a small guy by any means, but I was fully aware of my size, and if I needed to use it to get this guy off my property, I had no problem with that. "The weekly phone calls and messages you've left have given me a pretty good idea of what it is you want, and it's not happening. So why don't you head on back to the city before it realizes you're gone and shuts down?"

Maxwell's jaw twitched, and I had the feeling he was biting his tongue so he wouldn't lash out the way I know I would've if I were in his position. I wasn't in the mood to waste his time, or mine, though, and I turned on my heel and headed up the porch stairs.

"Wait."

I glanced over my shoulder to see Maxwell sigh and cross his arms over his chest.

"Can you at least point me in the direction of a hotel?"

"Why?"

"Because you people don't know how to salt a road, and I'd rather not risk my life on an icy turn."

Smirking, I turned back to Maxwell and pretended to think that over. "I'm guessing you'll want something five-star? Four at the least? Something with a full bar and one of those soft robes they give you."

The relief on his face almost sent me over the edge as he nodded. "That would be perfect."

"I bet it would. Pity you won't find one within a couple

hundred miles of here. Good luck, though." I started back up the stairs when Maxwell's grunt of frustration sounded behind me.

"Fine. What about a three-star?"

I let out a whistle. "You don't mind slummin' it for the night?"

"If I have to. I mean, I'll have to check for bedbugs because you never know with these places, but—"

"Let me stop you right there," I said, whirling around again. "Merrihill isn't exactly a tourist spot, and that's the way we like it. You won't find so much as a side-of-the-road motel around here, so put on your big-boy pants and drive back to New York."

Maxwell had the good grace to look properly put in his place. "I wasn't trying to be offensive—"

"Yet you managed to be anyway. Congratulations. Now if you don't mind, I have things I need to do around here before it gets dark."

I kicked the underside of my boots against the top landing of the porch and, once the snow was free, reached for the screen door.

"You're really going to make me drive home through a blizzard—in the *dark*?"

I gritted my teeth and prayed for patience as my fingers tightened on the handle. This guy couldn't have chosen a worse time to show up on my front doorstep. With the Christmas tree farm now open, I didn't have time to coddle some city boy—let alone a pain-in-my-*ass* city boy— who had done nothing but give me a headache since he discovered my phone number.

"I'm not *making* you do anything." I turned back to see

him standing at the bottom of my stairs. "You are the one who invited yourself up here, and *you* are the one who picked today of all days to drive out into the country. Maybe you should've thought about something other than lining your pockets before you got in a car that's not winterized and decided to drive through that blizzard you just mentioned."

There. Let him chew on that.

I turned, about to fling open my door, when I heard, "Wow... And you think *I'm* an asshole."

The vein at the side of my temple pulsed as I froze and counted back from ten. But around eight, I heard footsteps trudging up the stairs behind me.

"Look, I know you hate me and want me gone, but if I leave now I'm likely going to kill myself or someone else. Do you really want that on your conscience?"

I let out a sigh, because damn it, he was right. There was no way I could—in good conscience—let him head out with the snowstorm I knew was coming tonight. But it'd been easy enough to forget that when I was focused on how damn irritating he was.

"Fine."

"Fine?"

I reached for the screen door and yanked it open so hard I was surprised it didn't fly off the hinges.

"Fine, you can stay here." I shoved open the wooden door to the cabin. "But you get in my way or piss me off in any way, I'm tossing your ass out quicker than you can say 'bah humbug.'"

MAXWELL

CONSIDERING I'D PUT my foot in my mouth more than once since meeting Micah Noble, it came as a surprise when he offered to put me up in his own home. Then again, he could've saved me this trip by just agreeing to Willett-Goss's terms, so really it was his own damn fault I was here in the first place—and now stranded.

He didn't hold the entry open for me to enter, and I caught the handle just before the door slammed shut after him.

This should be fun.

I stepped inside the cabin and almost sighed as a wave of warmth enveloped me. It got cold in the city, but I only ever had to walk from the entrance of a building to a car, so this shit up here was ridiculous.

How do people live like this?

"It's not the Waldorf-Astoria, but it'll keep you from freezing to death outside."

He wasn't wrong about that. The five-star accommodations, not the freezing part, though I'd take my chances. This place wasn't anything you'd see in the city, from the log-cabin-type walls to the roaring fire in the small living room, where a pile of quilts sat on the arm of the lone couch. Beside it was an oversized recliner that was currently being occupied by a dog of some sort with droopy eyes and Dumbo-sized ears. It looked up as I entered the room, blinked, and then closed its eyes again, and I snorted.

"Some guard you have there. What is it?"

"What is it? You don't have dogs in the city?"

"Not ones that look like that."

Micah crossed his arms over his thick chest and looked like he was struggling not to roll his eyes. "Snoopy's a basset hound and he's got a mean bite, so leave him alone."

A mean bite? That lazy thing? Yeah, right.

"You can stay up here," Micah said, heading up the stairs to the second floor, fully expecting me to follow. Which I did. Only because I was curious about the kind of room I'd be sleeping in, not because I followed anyone else's orders.

The hallway he led me down was narrow and pretty much identical to the outside of the house. Wood logs with gnarly knots lined the way, and as I trailed behind my hulking host, I couldn't help but wonder if he'd chopped down the trees that built this place.

He came to a stop at the end of the hall, pushed open one of the doors, and stood aside. "This'll be you."

I peered around the corner and into the small room, where a narrow bed was pushed up against one wall and a wooden chest sat at the end of it with a patchwork quilt folded on top of it. I walked inside and did a quick 360, and felt my claustrophobia creeping in on me.

Yes, I lived in the city, where narrow spaces were the norm for most. But I'd worked my ass off to afford much more than a tiny hovel of a dwelling, and this just felt like a step in the wrong direction.

There was barely enough room for me to get changed in—not that I planned to get undressed anytime soon—but if Mr. Muscle over there were to stretch his arms out, I'd bet money he'd be able to touch both walls.

I glanced at the bed again. "Is this a single?"

Micah raised a brow. "It's a bed. You got a problem with it, you can always sleep out in the barn."

Before I could respond, Micah turned on his heel and started to walk away. I let out a breath and thought about just shutting the door and holing up in this...*room* until the storm passed, but I quickly nixed that idea and rushed out after Micah instead.

He was halfway back to the stairs when he said, "Bathroom's in there. There's only one, so don't take all night, and be careful with the hot water tap—it's fiddly."

"Fiddly as in...?"

"As in if you aren't careful the handle won't be the only thing that falls off; so will your freezing balls."

"This place just gets better and better."

"Hey, you're the one who invited yourself out here."

Micah pushed off the doorframe, and just as he was about to turn away from me I grabbed his arm—and Jesus, the thing was the size of a tree trunk.

He glanced down at my hand, and I quickly let go.

"There a problem?" he asked.

"No, I was just— There's no other bedroom up here. Where do you sleep?"

"Why? You want someone to cuddle with?"

"*No.*" My denial was as instantaneous as it was strong. But I had to admit, if he wasn't the man I'd been arguing with for the last several months, and he hadn't been such an ass today, I might've been tempted.

"Good. 'Cause that costs extra." He strode down the stairs, leaving me standing there with my mouth hanging open, and that was when I realized he hadn't answered my question.

"Let me guess," I said, following. "You prefer the barn you mentioned?"

"Not a bad option right about now."

"What's that supposed to mean?"

Micah whirled around without any warning, causing me to run into his chest face-first.

Yep. Solid muscle. He'd owe me a nose job if I'd just cracked the damn thing.

As I reached up to rub the bridge, Micah scowled. "Do you plan on following me around all night?"

"You act like I *want* to be here."

"Well, you are the one who drove onto my property when I was looking forward to a nice, quiet evening. Alone."

"And I'd be happy to leave you alone once I get what I came for."

Micah's eyes dropped to where I was still rubbing my nose. "A concussion?"

"I'd prefer a signature. Along with an understanding that—"

"God, here we go." With a groan, Micah stomped down the rest of the stairs and toward the kitchen.

"Would it kill you to have a conversation that could change your life? Give you all the money you need so you can get out of this place and—"

"You think I give a shit about money? This is my home. I'll sell it over my cold, dead body."

I nodded at the fireplace. "And if that goes out, I'm sure it'll happen."

"Nah, I've got enough firewood to last the next few months. And I can also throw you in it if I run out."

"Is that a threat?"

"Course not. Just making conversation." With the toe of his boot, Micah kicked out a chair from under the small dining table. "Sit if you're hungry."

"You're going to cook for me?"

"Leftover rabbit stew sound good?"

"Rabbit...?" I could feel the bile rise in my throat, taking over any feelings of hunger I may have had. "I think I'll pass."

A snort of laughter escaped Micah as he turned off the burner where a large pot had been simmering. "Don't worry, city boy. It's just homemade vegetable soup with regular beef. Nothing crazy."

To trust or not to trust, that was the question.

When I hesitated, my growling stomach made the decision for me, and I sat at the table as Micah ladled soup into bowls.

The kitchen was as...quaint as the rest of the house, with a single-door fridge, gas stove, and apron-style sink. That was it. There was no dishwasher, no center island, just the basics to get by with. I supposed the fact he had a fridge and stove were a step up in his world, though, because I wouldn't have been surprised if he'd been cooking the stew over an open flame.

"So, uh, how long have you lived here?" I asked as I took another look around the tight kitchen and living room, and judging by the worn floorboards and well-lived-in couch, I would guess awhile.

"My whole life."

"Your *whole* life, as in—"

"Was born out in the barn." Micah paused and looked over his shoulder with a smirk. "So I guess you could say I *have* slept in there."

I tried my hardest to keep my jaw from hitting the table, but *come on*. "You were born in a *barn?*"

"It's not as uncommon as you think around here. A couple of us were born in that barn."

"Us?"

"My brother and sisters," he said, bringing the bowls over to the table. "Us Nobles have lived and died on this land for generations."

Which was why he was being so damn obstinate about selling the place.

Okay, well, at least I knew the reason behind his stubborn resolve. I'd known it had to be something like that, because only a complete moron would turn down the kind of cash we were offering.

A complete moron *or* a sentimental one.

"You want anything to drink?"

"Sure, I'll take a water." When he grabbed a glass out of one of the cabinets and turned on the tap, I quickly interrupted, "Or do you maybe have something in the fridge?"

I should've known he wouldn't have the bottled kind.

Micah flicked off the faucet, walked over to the fridge, pulled it open, and held up a beer. I screwed my nose up.

"It's this or milk."

"I suppose that's freshly milked from your own cows?"

Micah's lips twitched. "I don't own cows."

"I think I'll pass."

He shrugged and kicked the door shut, then flicked off the top of the beer he held. As he straddled the chair and pulled it in under the table, I picked up the soup spoon he'd handed me and stirred my stew.

"So I gotta ask," Micah said before he took a swig of his beer. "Because I've been scratching my head trying to figure this out, and after *meeting* you, I'm even more baffled. What's a guy like you want so badly with my tree farm?"

"I don't want the farm."

Micah narrowed his eyes, and my fingers tightened on the spoon I held.

"What I mean is, Willett-Goss is interested in the property. The land itself. Not the business."

"Why? It's not like there's oil here, or anything worth the kind of money you've been throwing my way. What could some bigwig company from the city want with this out-of-the-way lot? There's nothing here."

I grinned and pointed at him. "Exactly. And from what you said to me earlier, nothing for miles for anyone looking for a place to stay."

"Meaning?"

"*Meaning* we see an opportunity here. A big opportunity to reinvigorate the area. To bring life and families, tourists from all over to this part of the state, and where would they stay?"

"I'm almost afraid to ask," Micah muttered.

"At the five-star resort we build for them." I was really getting into it now, so much so I'd forgotten the growling animal inhabiting my stomach as I put my spoon back on the table and waved my hand like my vision would magically appear. "Imagine a grand cabin." I turned and looked into the living room, where I could see snow falling outside the window. "Kind of like yours, but on a much bigger and fancier scale—"

"Of course…"

"It would have roaring fireplace in the lobby, spa and sauna services, massages, and a bar to get a hot toddy at. With the snow falling outside and the crackling warmth enveloping you on the inside, it would be like a winter dream."

When I finished my spiel I saw Micah staring at me, his head cocked to one side. "You seem to forget that winter dream of yours comes at my dream's expense."

I opened my mouth to tell him that wasn't true, that he'd make off with so much money he could have *any* dream. But before I could get a word out, he held up his hand.

"Did it ever occur to you that this town doesn't want or need a big, fancy resort in it? That the people here don't want that."

"Who wouldn't want it? The local businesses? Come

on, you know just as well as I do they would profit from the people coming here."

Micah shook his head. "You don't understand. People like you never do. All you think about is money, money, money. What about community? Knowing your neighbor? Having a place where you belong?"

Is this guy serious? Who the hell thinks about that anymore?

"That might be how *you* think. But I bet if you asked the other residents of Merrihill, they'd love what we're proposing."

"And I think if you'd deigned to set a foot in this town before today, you'd know how wrong you are. Maybe if you bothered to actually get to know a place before you tear it to the ground, you'd understand there's more to life than lining your pockets." Micah stuck his spoon in his bowl and scooped up a heaping helping of his meal. "The answer is no, and if you don't eat your dinner soon, it's going to go cold."

Okay, then, I guessed the conversation was over...for now.

MICAH

S WAS MY daily routine, I was up and at 'em before the sun rose, bringing in armfuls of wood, since it was gonna be another cold one and I needed to keep the fire stoked.

I'd always enjoyed quiet mornings, the peace that came with a strong cup of coffee and the crackling of the embers. Even now as I sat on the couch looking over a checklist for the tree farm's annual barn dance that weekend, I reveled in it, enjoying the lack of phones ringing and the hustle and bustle I'd experienced on my rare trips to the city.

Which, in turn, made me wonder if the Scrooge upstairs was getting the best sleep of his life without all the noise or if the cacophony of traffic and horns was necessary. I glanced over at the stairs and listened intently, but he wasn't stirring a bit.

Just as well. With the amount of snow that had fallen overnight, he wouldn't be going anywhere anytime soon.

I took another sip of my coffee, smiling to myself as the sweetness of the snow cream hit my tongue. Usually just a couple of drops of milk was all I preferred, but snow cream during the holidays had always been a tradition, and definitely one that city boy Scrooge should enjoy while he was here.

After hearing his intent for my family's land last night, I wasn't exactly looking forward to another conversation about how he planned to tear down trees to build luxury accommodations for a bunch of tourists no one in this town wanted. It was one thing to tell him, though, and another thing for him to see it.

And Maxwell Scott was going to have to see for himself to believe.

The sound of the floor creaking overhead alerted me to my unwanted guest waking, and I headed to the kitchen for a caffeine refill.

"You gonna move?" I looked down to where Snoopy sat on the kitchen mat in front of the coffee pot, his dopey eyes even more so from the disturbance to his sleep. "You're a lazy lump, you know that, right?"

He let out a loud yawn, his jowls hanging low, as he rested his head back on his paws.

"Okay...guess I'll work around you."

I leaned over to grab the coffee pot, and just as I finished topping it off, I turned to see Scrooge standing in the doorway of the kitchen.

Huh, he'd managed to put himself together awfully quick considering I'd just heard him get up. He had his leather shoes perfectly buffed and tied, his suit was all back in place, and his hair was slightly damp from where I assumed he'd smoothed it down.

The only indication he was anything other than one hundred percent put together was the faint shadow now lining his cheeks, and the few wrinkles I could spot in his pant legs.

I walked over to the fridge to get some more of the snow cream and, after adding it to my coffee, leaned up against the door, giving him another once-over.

"Mornin'. What'd you do? Sleep in your clothes?"

Maxwell looked down at himself and ran his hands over his lapels. "No—well, not the jacket. What else was I going to sleep in? It's not like I planned this little overnighter, and I wasn't going to sleep nak—"

"Naked?" My lips curled up at the sides. "What? Too rustic for you? Too *free*?" I nodded. "Yeah, I can see that. You're too uptight to just bare it all."

Maxwell took a step forward, straightening his shoulders. "I'm not uptight."

I pushed off the fridge and went to walk by him but stopped when we were shoulder to shoulder. Then I looked down at his perfectly styled hair. "Whatever you say, Max."

As I continued into the living room, he whirled around. "My name's Max*well*."

I scoffed and stopped by the front window, staring out at the snow falling. "And you say you're not uptight."

"I'm not, but Max is not my name."

Not bothered in the least by his irritation, I shrugged. "It is while you're here, which, by the way, might be longer than you think."

"What? Why?"

I gestured to the row of snow-covered pines, then looked over my shoulder to him. "What, are you really prepared to drive in that?"

Max walked up to stand beside me at the window and shook his head, his denial strong as he marched off toward the front door and pulled it open.

Damn, the man was on a mission, and I couldn't help but laugh as I wondered if it was me or this place he was trying to run from.

"I wouldn't advise going that fast in those shoes," I said, smirking as he tore down the stairs, holding on to the rail for dear life.

"Nobody asked you." As Max reached the bottom of the porch stairs, he fished his keys out of his pocket and headed toward the carport he'd parked under. Doing so had meant he didn't have the feet of snow on his hood, but that wouldn't matter much.

"So you're just gonna leave? Before the sun's come up? What happened to all that determination I saw yesterday?"

"Oh, it's still there. I'm determined to find a hotel with a bed big enough that my feet don't hang over the edge. And then I'm determined to come back here when you've had some time to think over my offer and come to your senses."

"You found a hotel that lives up to your high standards? Around here?"

"No, but I'm sure I can." Max tried to wrench the frozen car door open, and I hid a grin behind my hand as I watched the struggle. "I want a hot breakfast, an even hotter shower, and then I'll be back, so don't even think about going anywhere."

With a final tug, the door swung open, almost knocking Max off his feet. When he regained his balance, he buttoned his suit jacket and smoothed a hand over his dark hair, attempting to compose himself while I attempted not to laugh my ass off.

He slid into the car, slammed the door shut, and then...nothing.

For a good two minutes I watched as Scrooge tried to get the car started, but the poor guy didn't seem to be having any luck. That wasn't shocking, nor was the mad-as-hell expression on his face when he finally gave up and got out of the car.

He marched over to where I stood under the cover of the porch and glared at me.

"What did you do to my car?"

"Excuse me?"

"It won't even start. It was fine yesterday."

"And that's my fault how?"

Max's jaw twitched as he seemed to try to come up with a good reason, but when nothing came out of his mouth, I chuckled.

"You think I'm trying to keep you here? I didn't realize city boys had a sense of humor."

"Well, whatever it is you did, it's not gonna work." He held his hand out. "So why don't you give me your keys instead?"

I blinked, waiting for him to laugh or throw out another smartass remark, but the guy was dead serious. "You want me to let you take my car? It's not enough that you want to steal my land, my entire life, but now my car? You've lost your damn mind."

"I already told you I'm coming back—"

"What don't you understand about this situation, Max? It's obvious you're not going anywhere, so instead of begging for what you can't have, you should really be kissing my ass to let you stay until you can get your car fixed."

"I understand this situation just fine. Last night my car worked and this morning it is not. The only person out here is you, and—"

About done with this conversation, I shook my head and turned to march back toward the house.

"Hey! Where are you going? I was in the middle of talking."

"And I was at the end of caring. So if you have anything else to say, tell it to one of my trees."

I stomped up the stairs, the snow falling off my boots as I went, and as I pulled open the door, I heard Max coming up behind me.

"Okay, fine, you didn't mess with my car. But you can't blame me for being suspicious."

I grabbed my coat off the rack and shrugged into it. I needed to get started on my day, and standing here arguing with Maxwell Scott wasn't going to do my chores for me.

"I can blame you for whatever the hell I want. First"—I took a step forward, backing him up a step—"you drive up here uninvited. Second"—I took another step, making him bump into the wall—"you get marooned out here due to bad weather. And third—"

I stopped when we were toe to toe. The pompous ass

was looking up at me, and somewhere around there, I lost my train of thought.

Max glared at me, those brown eyes flashing as he angled his chin in defiance. "And third, what?"

My eyes dropped to his lips as he spoke, and when I didn't immediately answer he licked his lower one.

Wait, why am I even looking at his lips?

I took a step back and shook my head. "*Third*, you're a bossy, ungrateful rich guy who thinks everyone will bow down to him. Well I got news for you, Scrooge: you might be king of the city where everyone does whatever you want, but me? I bow to no one."

WHAT AN INFURIATING, judgmental, stupidly gorgeous, utterly ridiculous man.

And for some reason that combination had me more intrigued than I could remember being in a long time, even with as put out as I currently felt.

Stranded up in Nowheresville... See, this was when a luxury resort would've come in handy. I wouldn't be complaining if that were the case. A glass of expensive scotch, a deep-tissue massage, and a feast of lobster and wagyu beef would go a long way to making me forget about snow up to my knees and the fact that my car hated the weather as much as I did.

Micah was still glaring at me, and though he'd said he wasn't the kind of guy who would do whatever I wanted, I was still determined to get what I came here for. After all this, there was no way I was heading back to the firm without a signed deal in hand.

"You think you could at least give me the number for someone who can fix my car?" I said.

"Gladly." Micah flipped open a notepad on the kitchen table and scribbled out a number. "Her name's Emily."

"*Her* name?"

"You got a problem with that?"

"Not as long as she can fix my car." I pulled my cell phone out of my pocket and went to dial the mechanic's number, but there was no signal. "You don't have cell towers out here?"

Micah shrugged. "Guess not."

"Then how do you call someone?"

"With this mind-blowing invention called"—he walked past me and pointed to the landline on the wall—"a phone."

"I didn't know people still used those."

"Wow. You really are some kind of spoiled, aren't you?"

With a roll of my eyes, I grabbed the receiver and dialed the number he'd written down. The phone rang several times before a woman picked up. "Emily, whatcha need?"

"Hello, I need your assistance to fix my Lexus this morning."

There was a long pause and then, "Who is this?"

"My name is Maxwell Scott and I'm stranded at the Noble residence—"

"Ahh, makes sense now."

"What does?"

"No one in Merrihill would be caught dead driving a Lexus."

"Excuse me?"

"Not a very practical ride out here. So what's the problem?"

I clenched my molars. "If I knew what the problem was, I wouldn't be calling you, now would I?"

"Testy. You say you're a friend of the Nobles?"

"We're not friends, and that's besides the point. Can you fix my car or not?"

"Sure I can. When I get back."

"What time will that be?"

"I dunno, maybe early afternoon—"

"That'll do—"

"—on the twenty-sixth."

I blinked, not comprehending for a long moment. "You mean today. This afternoon."

"No, I mean the twenty-sixth. The shop's closed for the holidays, and even if it weren't, I can't get a part for a Lexus till after Christmas."

My mouth fell open as my brain tried to comprehend what she was saying, and when nothing came out, Micah reached out and took the phone.

"Hey there, Em." He paused for a minute and listened to whatever this Emily woman was telling him, then chuckled. "Yeah, I think he's trying to process what you just told him. That or he's about to pass out." Micah ran his eyes over me and smirked. "He does look a little pale. So, the twenty-sixth, you say?"

My eyes widened as Micah repeated the same horrible words she had said to me a minute ago.

"Hmm, that's not the best news I've heard all week—"

Ah, no shit.

"—but I guess he can use the spare room here a little longer."

Is he kidding right now? There is no way I'm spending another night here.

Micah nodded, said a couple more things I didn't bother listening to, then hung up the phone. I walked into the tiny living room and looked out at the snow blanketing the ground outside.

I was stuck.

Stranded here.

Out in the middle of nowhere.

And all I wanted to do was scream.

"Well, looks like you're stuck here."

I sucked in a breath and tried to tell myself it could be worse. But when I turned to face the smug bastard behind me, I couldn't for the life of me work out how.

"Way to point out the obvious there."

Micah crossed his arms and gave a lazy shrug. "Nah, just the irony. Here you are wanting to buy up the place so you can demolish it and build your log cabin dream, yet you can't wait to get away from it."

"As it currently stands."

"Ouch, well, that's just rude. Not to mention kind of offensive. If I were you, I'd be a little nicer to me, considering I am your only option right now."

Okay, so maybe he had a point. I needed to rein my frustration in and try to remember why I was here. Maybe I could turn this into a good thing, find a silver lining. I was out here to try to convince Micah to sign his property over to me, so maybe I could use this forced proximity to work a little magic.

"You're right." I slipped my hands into my pockets and tried not to look at the scuffed floorboards and couch that had seen better days, as I crossed back over to Micah. "I didn't mean to come off as rude—"

"Really? Because it sure sounded like it."

"Look, I'm trying to apologize here."

Micah let out a sigh and ran a hand through the sexy strands of hair that had fallen in his face. "Fair point."

"I'm just a little frustrated at the whole car situation, that's all."

"You sure that's it?"

"Well, that and I don't have any clothes other than what I'm wearing for the next however many days."

Micah ran his eyes over me again, much like he had when he was talking to Emily the mechanic. But something about his perusal this time had my body heating. It was slower, more deliberate, and when he finally reached my face, he licked his lips in a way that made my cock jerk.

"I'm sure I could find something for you to wear around here during your stay."

I swallowed and readjusted my pants, thanking God that my hands were already in my pockets. "Uh, I don't know…"

"It's either that or be prepared to attract a grizzly or two."

"As in a *bear*?"

Micah snorted. "I mean, several days in those clothes and you're gonna smell like a dead animal."

Horrified, I let my mouth fall open, and Micah—the sexy bastard—just laughed.

"Come with me, Max. Let's find something so you don't become bear bait."

He headed toward the stairs, and I quickly followed after him—and with the view I had going up the stairs, all thoughts of bear attacks left my head.

Micah Noble had one fine ass—something he more than likely knew, since he wrapped it in denim probably ninety-five percent of his life—and it was all I could do not to reach out and grab it.

Again, very grateful my hands were in my pockets.

"Right," he said, and walked back into the room I'd tried to sleep in last night. "Let's see what we've got." He opened one of the dresser drawers, pulled out a handful of neatly folded boxer briefs, and tossed them on the bed. When my eyes widened, he snickered. "Don't worry. They're clean."

"You know, maybe just clothes would be fine. I don't need—"

"Yeah, you do. Unless you want to literally freeze your balls off. Up to you."

I snapped my mouth shut. I probably needed those.

Micah added a few t-shirts and pajama pants to the pile before moving to the closet. An assortment of jeans, long johns, and flannel shirts took up the small space, and he indiscriminately grabbed enough to last me the next few days.

I held up one of the flannel shirts, seeing instantly that it was going to swallow me whole, but there wasn't a lot I could do about that. After all, it wasn't like I chopped wood for a living to gain biceps the size of tree trunks.

"There a problem?" Micah crossed his arms, looking a little defensive as he watched me go through his clothes.

"Yeah, there is," I said, tossing the flannel on the bed. "Why are you being so nice to me?"

"And I thought I was giving you shit earlier."

"You were. But this...and giving me a place to crash. Why would you do that if you don't want to?"

Micah narrowed his eyes like he was trying to suss out if I was joking or not, but when I cocked my head and waited for his answer, he sighed.

"Look, that's what we do out here. We don't just leave someone in the lurch, entitled city boy or not." He nodded at the clothes. "See if any of that works. If not, maybe you can make a toga out of the bedsheets."

As he closed the bedroom door behind him, I bit down on my lip, wondering how it was that someone I barely knew could make me feel the slight bit of guilt that was creeping in.

But what did I have to feel guilty about? I was going to make this man so much money he could sleep on stacks of hundred-dollar bills if he wanted to. So if he felt put out at the moment over helping me, that was a small price to pay for ensuring a wealthy future.

He really should be thanking me.

MICAH

’D BREWED ANOTHER full pot of coffee for the impending wild crew, also known as my family, that would be heading my way soon to get things ready for the tree farm tonight. Unlike other sellers, we only opened our gates twice a week, making it an event for the town by including a few fun extras along with shopping for their special tree. It wasn't anything Max would've seen before, and I was curious what he'd think of it all.

For now, though, he was content to grumble under his breath as he made his way down the stairs, fiddling with the ends of the green flannel shirt he wore—one that fit me well but hung down to his thighs.

"I look ridiculous," he said as he stepped into the kitchen and gave me a look that said he wasn't impressed. Of course he wasn't. It wasn't tailored or worth at least four figures.

"You'll stay warm. That's what matters."

"Before or after I die of shame?" He grabbed on to the

waist of his jeans as they slid down his hips, and I bit back a grin.

"Wait here." I headed into my bedroom and a few seconds later returned with a leather belt. "This should keep them up."

"Great. What an appealing ensemble." Max lifted up his shirt to thread the belt through the pant loops, and as he did, I caught sight of his taut abs and the waistband of the boxer briefs I'd loaned him. Something about seeing his smooth, hairless skin in comparison to my own and the fact that he was wearing something intimate that belonged to me...it made my body react in a way I hadn't expected, and I found myself needing to move behind the counter to hide the evidence.

The last thing I wanted was for Max to catch me giving his body a long perusal, so I averted my eyes by focusing back on my coffee.

Max continued to grumble as he tucked in his shirt, then decided to untuck it, then changed his mind again and pushed just the front ends behind the waist of the jeans.

"Look at you. A proper lumberjack," I said, smirking behind my mug. "Ready to chop wood?"

Scrooge's eyes widened. "You have *got* to be kidding me."

"I thought you enjoyed the heat? Wouldn't want the fires to die out now, would you?"

"I'm not here for manual labor. That's your kink, not mine."

Such a smartass mouth. I wondered how that went over with his former lovers.

Not that I was thinking about his former lovers. Or him with others. Or him at all.

Jesus.

"I'd say consider it your lucky day, since I've got enough of a stockpile and won't need to see you accidentally chop off one of your limbs, but I have a feeling you might prefer that to what's coming. Or should I say who."

"You mean you actually get visitors out here? What do they do, ride a sleigh over?"

"Some of them do."

"*Some* of them?"

"Mhmm. My brother and sisters. They help run the place you want to tear down." I took a sip of my coffee and shrugged. "Thought you might want to try your pitch with them, since you're getting nowhere with me."

Max's eyes widened, and I had to admit, it felt good getting one up on him—even if I was bullshitting him.

"Seriously?"

I nodded, biting back a laugh. *Yeah, how's it feel to be put on the spot?*

"You want me to pitch my business plan to your family wearing *this*?" He gestured to his outfit again, and that was when I realized he was more worried about his clothes than actually telling my siblings he wanted to bulldoze their family home to the ground.

"That's what you're worried about?"

He looked at me as though I'd lost my mind. "Of course. How is anyone going to take me seriously in this?"

Unbelievable...

He turned to head back to the stairs, and just as he

reached the bottom one, the sound of booted feet on the front porch caught my attention before—

"Hey, Micah!"

—my brother Travis threw open the front door and walked on in.

"Your lazy ass sleep in or somethin'? Your drive is a damn snowfield out there. You forget where you put the plow?"

"Mornin' to you too, Travis." I made my way around the kitchen counter and met my brother in the middle of the living room. "Come on in."

"Don't mind if I do. You got some coffee brewin'?" My brother shrugged out of his thick weather-proof jacket and threw it over the end of the couch before brushing past me and heading toward the kitchen.

I looked over to where Max had frozen at the bottom of the stairs, his eyes following the lumbering jackass who'd just barged in. Travis was a good inch or so taller than I was —yep, us Noble men were made from hearty stock—and I wondered if Max was reconsidering his plan to try pitching my family.

"You got any snow cream left?" Travis asked as he filled a mug and then pulled open the fridge. "No? Man, you really are slackin' this morning."

"I'm sorry. I've been a little busy," I finally said.

I was about to explain I had an unexpected guest when my sister, Gina, opened the door and stopped inside the doorway, brushing snow off her shoulders.

"Would you get your ass in here and close the door? What were you, born in a barn?" I said.

"Actually..." She flashed a wide grin at the inside joke

because, well, she *had* been born in the barn, just like me. "What are you so grumbly about? You said come over early."

"I know, but with all this opening and shutting of the door, you're letting all the warm air out. I suppose Taylor and Lana are out there too? Why can't you all ever arrive at once?"

"We did," Gina said, unwinding the scarf she had knotted at her neck. "But when the drive wasn't plowed, we sent Travis ahead with a shovel, and when we finally got up here, we spotted some fancy-ass rich car parked under the carport. What moron drove that out here?"

When I glanced over at Max, Travis and Gina's attention followed, and for the first time since they'd arrived, there was dead silence.

For all of about ten seconds, because then Taylor and Lana bounded inside, bringing what seemed like a foot of snow with them.

"Would it kill you to kick off your boots—" I started, but Gina had zeroed in on Max and taken a step toward him.

"So *you're* the moron," she said.

Taylor's head jerked in our direction. "Who's a moron?"

"This guy." Gina nodded toward the out-of-place visitor in our midst. "Didn't you see the ridiculous car outside?" She snorted. "What'd you do, get stuck out here?"

"Who got stuck?" With Snoopy blocking her path, Lana tripped and fell face-first onto the floor, but with her heavily padded jackets, she didn't seem to feel a thing. Instead she blew a long strand of hair out of her face to see what we were all looking at, and when she caught sight of Max, she frowned. "Who the hell are you?"

"The moron," Travis clarified. "Apparently."

Max's jaw was clenched tight, and I fully expected him to go off on my siblings in the same way he'd done with me. But something must've clicked in his head—maybe the fact that he needed to win them over to his way of thinking, because he forced a smile.

"I'm afraid we haven't been properly introduced. I'm Maxwell Scott, and you must be the rest of the Noble family? It's a pleasure to finally meet you."

Taylor raised a brow at me. "Is he your boyfriend?"

"Micah wouldn't date someone who drives without snow tires," Gina said.

Travis snorted out a laugh. "I don't think Micah dates, period."

"All right, all right, all of you can shut up now," I said. "Max here is from the company that wants to raze our house so they can put up a shopping mall—"

"A resort hotel, actually," Max interrupted.

"Same thing. And too bad for him his city car doesn't seem to want to work in the snow, so it looks like he'll be here for a few days. Aren't we lucky?"

The wide eyes and dropped jaws from each of my siblings was a fun sight, especially when they turned from me back to Max and their gazes turned heated.

Ah. This was entertainment at its best. Who needed a fancy resort for that?

"Look, as much as I'd love to watch you try to charm these four, we have work to do. You can either sit in here with Snoopy or join us outside. There's a coat up in the closet of the spare room that should fit."

"Like a blanket, maybe," Travis muttered, making me laugh.

"Okay, that's enough out of you four. Get outside and help me plow the drive—as you've already pointed out, I'm running a little behind this morning."

Taylor pulled open the door, aiming another glare Max's way. "I suppose we have him to thank for that too."

"Just go," I said as I placed mine and Travis's empty coffee mugs in the sink.

As I followed Travis to the door, I noticed Max still standing at the bottom of the stairs, his eyes focused on the four who'd just left the house.

"There a problem? You need something else?"

"No, I..." He shook his head and brought his attention back to me. "That was just a lot." When I frowned, he was quick to add, "I mean, there's a *lot* of you."

"Uh huh." I stepped out the door and grabbed the handle. "Spare room closet. You can't miss it."

I pulled the door shut, and when I turned around found all four of my siblings at the bottom of the stairs looking up at me, curious and skeptical looks on their faces.

"Sure he's not your boyfriend?" Taylor asked as I started down the stairs.

"Some fancy city boy, huh?" Travis shoved my arm and shot me a goofy grin. "Wouldn't have expected that from you."

"Because *that* isn't what's going on. I told you, he's from—"

"That piece-of-shit company that wants to take our land."

I glanced over at Gina, whose brows were practically hitting her hairline with her indignation, then frowned.

"Yes, that's right, but I feel like he has a vision and I get that. I just don't want him to have it here."

Okay...why in the hell did I suddenly feel the need to stick up for Maxwell friggin' Scott?

"A vision?" Lana scoffed as we continued toward the barn. "What is he? A psychic or something? Anyone with half a brain can see that this place is exactly as it should be. Snow-covered trees, sparkling lights, sleigh rides, and Christmas music. This place is magical at night. Maybe he just needs to stick around a little longer to see it."

I couldn't help my grin as I unlatched the lock on the barn and pulled open the heavy door, and as they all walked inside out of the snow, I nodded. "My thoughts exactly."

The four of them stopped once they were inside and turned to face me, the *huh?* written all over their faces.

"You didn't actually think I was going to let him leave without seeing this place come alive, did you?"

Taylor blinked once, twice, and then... "You messed with his car."

I couldn't help the devious smile that hit my lips, because yep, I'd totally messed with his car. Sure, I'd denied it when Max accused me—and would until my dying day—but there was only one way to ensure he and his company would leave us alone for good, and that was for Scrooge himself to get an up-close-and-personal view of what made this place so special.

"Well, well, well," Gina said, throwing an arm around

my shoulders. "It looks like our golden boy has finally come over to the dark side. After all these years, our awesomeness has rubbed off on him."

"I think you mean your deviousness," I said. "I might've channeled you a bit. But this guy is something else. It'll do him good to learn the true value of this place."

Taylor side-eyed Lana. "Hmm. Did you hear what I just heard?"

"I did." Lana nodded, and then they both looked at me with mischievous grins. "This guy's something else, huh? Not too hard on the eyes... But I'm sure that has nothing to do with it. Micah would never fall for a city boy again."

"Nope, never," Taylor agreed. "Definitely not one trying to take away his home."

Exactly. That would be crazy. I'd only rigged his car for the purpose of keeping everything I held close. It didn't matter that Max was attractive. Or an ass.

Or that I kept watching the front door hoping he'd walked out of it.

Maxwell Scott was enemy number one, and that wasn't something I'd be forgetting just because sparring with him had made my body come alive.

MAXWELL

*H*OURS LATER AND my body felt like I'd been slung around a boxing ring all day. I should've stayed in front of the fire and napped like Snoopy. Instead, my curiosity had gotten the better of me and I'd become the bitch boy for the Noble siblings.

"Max, take this wheelbarrow of supplies over to Travis and watch out for the snowdrifts."

"Max, restring the lights that fell off the fence. No, not like that. Not like that, either."

"Max, go get the bags of marshmallows and graham crackers out of Gina's car and bring them half a mile down to the firepit."

This manual labor shit was not for me. This was not what I signed up for when I'd agreed to come up here. It wasn't in my nature to admit defeat, but I was getting mighty close to saying screw it and throwing in the towel on this whole thing.

No. This is a multimillion-dollar deal that could land you a partnership. Don't let a little snow and bossy fuckers run you off.

Tell that to my aching back and frostbitten toes.

I lowered myself slowly onto the couch to rest for a few minutes while the psycho siblings opened up the Christmas tree farm for the line of cars already waiting outside the gates.

Probably people they hired, I thought, stretching my fingers out to feel the warmth from the fire. No way did anyone willingly come out here to freeze and look at trees. Give me a break.

"All that work today and you're hiding in here for the show?"

Micah's voice had me glancing over my shoulder to see him heading toward his room.

"I'm not hiding," I called out. "I'm thawing."

A smirk crossed Micah's lips as he walked back into the room carrying a small locked box. "If you need another pair of long johns, you know where to find 'em."

"No thanks."

"You sure? I see how fragile you city boys are. I'd hate for you to lose a limb."

I jerked around and scowled. "That didn't seem to cross your mind when I was hauling your shit through the snow all day. Where was your concern then?"

"With the guests coming to visit the tree farm this evening. I'm sorry, did you expect the whole world to stop and worry about you? Remember, you are here of your own volition—"

"Big word."

"Yeah, funny, but I remember learning a few of those during my years at college."

My eyes widened. "*You* went to college?"

Micah took in a deep breath and made his way back to the middle of the living room, stopping in front of me so I had to crane my neck to look up at him.

"Do you try to be rude, or is it just a natural talent of yours?"

I opened my mouth, about to respond, but he held a hand up, shushing me.

"I don't actually need you to answer, since I've got plenty of evidence to make my own deduction, but I guess I'm just curious. Do know how offensive that mouth of yours is?"

I reared back into the couch, bringing my fingers up to said mouth.

"It just talks and talks without thinking." His eyes dropped to where I was touching my lower lip, and he narrowed them. "Makes me wonder what else it would do without thinking."

I blinked, trying to switch gears from insult to innuendo, because that had most *definitely* been an innuendo. But before I could say anything, Micah turned on his heel and headed for the door.

After he pulled it open, he stopped in the doorway and glanced back over his shoulder to where I still sat with my back plastered to the couch and my jaw in my lap.

"The problem with you city guys is you never know when to shut up." He ran his eyes down over me and then shook his head. "And the problem with me is that I want to make you."

My cock hardened at the heat in his eyes, even as he admonished me, and as he stormed out the door, I was happy to note that at least one of my appendages was definitely not suffering from frostbite—my dick was hard as a rock.

What the hell was the matter with it? Every time Micah insulted me, the stupid thing got excited, and I'd be damned if he walked out of here thinking he was leaving me all tongue-tied and turned on.

I gave my wayward friend a stern talking-to, and once I was decent, I threw back on my jacket and gloves and marched over to the door, determined to track down Micah and tell him he needed to stop with these back-handed compliments because they were confusing my poor cock.

But as I stepped outside, Micah had already disap-peared, his footprints in the snow leading toward the direc-tion of the tree farm.

Fine. Whatever. I'd go look at what he thought was such a big deal around here, but I wasn't lifting another finger or manning a booth. And forget about helping load any Christmas trees into trunks. The last thing I needed was splinters to join the frostbite.

As I kept to the plowed path that led behind the house and down to the tree farm, the sound of upbeat holiday music filled the air, along with voices laughing and the cheerful chatter of a crowd. From the vantage point of the hill, I was able to look down at the whole scene: now that night had fallen, it was a sea of white and multicolored lights stretching across several acres. On one side were trees planted neatly in rows, all of them at least six feet or more, with heavy branches and axes at the ready—because of course Micah wouldn't dream of chopping down anything that wouldn't be used.

Making my way down the hill, I passed the barn, where Taylor was handing out cider and hot chocolate, along with long skewers and s'mores kits so people could roast marshmallows along the handful of firepits set up.

"Watch out!" yelled a voice behind me, and I turned around just in time to jump out of the way of a speeding sled, driven by a maniacal kid with wild blond hair and a smattering of freckles. I wouldn't have noticed a thing about the little shit, though, if I hadn't lost my footing and ended up on my ass in the snow.

"Hey, you brat, why don't you watch where the hell you're going?"

"Yelling at kids now? I thought you saved your wrath for the likes of my brother." Travis gave a lopsided grin and held his hand out to help me up.

I ignored it. "That speed demon tried to run me over."

"Well, it helps if you stay out of the sledding lanes."

"The what?" As another sled raced past us, I looked up to where they were coming from. "Oh. There should be signs, then."

Travis pointed to a "Sledding in progress" sign. "Like that?"

Well, shit. I rolled my eyes and stalked off as Travis chuckled behind me.

It wasn't like I wasn't used to dodging crazy drivers during Christmas—hello, I worked near Rockefeller Center, for God's sake. A.k.a. the place everyone in the United States thought was necessary to visit during the holidays.

On second thought, maybe a stop at the barn for some spiked cider might not be a bad idea. I trudged through the snow, dusting my ass off as I went, and wondered just how spiked this cider would be. Knowing this bunch of merry men, probably a drop or two of the good stuff, and an overwhelming amount of apple, spices, and sugary-sweet stuff.

I mean, really, I'd heard of people getting in the Christmas spirit and all, but the Noble family was a whole other case study. Not only did they own a Christmas tree farm, they practically brought the holiday to life on it for a couple days a week for the *entire* month of December. They were either relatives of Santa or saints for sure—with a name like Noble, it could go either way, right?—because this much cheer made me want to gag.

I trudged up the side of the barn to the upbeat song of some overplayed Christmas tune, and wondered why they never mentioned the freezing fingers and wet asses that came from this time of the year. No, it was always holly jolly this and chestnuts roasting over open fires, but in reality no one wanted Jack Frost nipping at their nose.

I sighed and turned the corner to head into the barn, hoping some cider would thaw my frozen insides, and my eyes landed on the man I'd been in search of this whole miserable time. Micah was standing over by the table that held the warm cider and treats, and I was going to march right over there and give him a piece of my mind.

I went to take a step forward, and when my stupid boot caught on the bottom of the enormous pants I was wearing and I almost tripped, I let out a curse and crouched down to roll the damn things up.

Fine, I would march over there and give him a piece of my mind...in a minute.

I folded the wet fabric over on itself and kept my eyes glued to my target so he wouldn't get away again—not that it was hard, considering he was as tall as one of the trees outside. But as I switched to the other pant leg, I saw a handsome man in a grey peacoat walk up to Micah and tap him on one of his ridiculously large arms.

Micah turned, and when he saw who stood behind him, a wide smile curved his lips and his entire expression lit up.

Hmm, now what do we have here?

Unlike all the other locals here tonight, this man had an air of familiarity about him. In his fitted coat, black woolen pants, and leather shoes, he looked sophisticated, worldly, and one hundred percent "city." He looked as though he belonged in Manhattan, rushing down the street with a briefcase in hand. Not showing up at some small-town Christmas tree farm festivities.

Fascinated, I kept my eyes locked on the unlikely pair as I straightened to my full height and moved off to the side. All thoughts of cider and giving Micah a piece of my mind were now replaced by curiosity over who this man was, because he'd somehow transformed the scowling, overbearing jerk I knew into a gorgeous, sexy, *welcoming* host.

I inched closer, wondering if I could catch a glimpse of what they were saying, but with this blasted holiday music, I couldn't hear squat.

Just my luck—something interesting is finally happening here and I can't even listen in.

Micah grinned down at the man and reached out to dust some snow from his coat, and when Mr. Sophistication laughed and took Micah's hand in his to give it a squeeze, that urge to gag I'd had earlier returned, making my stomach twist.

What the hell? I rubbed a hand over my irritated stomach but kept close tabs on the two across the barn from me.

Micah nodded, tugged the man over to where the cider stand was, and grabbed one of the cups to fill it for him. So damn chivalrous, wasn't he? Where was *that* guy when my car broke down?

When Micah turned back, handing over the cup, Mr. Sophistication took it from him and purposely grazed their fingers together, *if* I was not mistaken—and I wasn't. I knew a longing look when I saw one. As Micah dropped his hand and turned back to fill his own cup, his companion all but had hearts in his eyes.

Huh, seemed like Micah liked to run over all the city boys' hearts, didn't he?

Wait...what?

I didn't mean me, *city boy, just whoever that was.* I certainly wouldn't let anyone run all over my heart...

"Hey, mister?"

A tugging on my arm snapped me out of my thoughts and pulled my attention away from the two across the barn. I looked down to see a bundled-up ball of wool and polyester standing beside me.

"What is it, kid?"

"Could you come and help me cut down my tree? I picked it out and know exactly which one I want."

I raised an eyebrow at this poor, delusional child. "I don't cut down trees."

The kid frowned, his red nose scrunching. "But Mom told me to come and find someone who works here."

Oh, hell no. *That* was the last straw. Time to give this kid a wake-up call.

I crouched down on his level so we were eye to eye. "Out of all these people, you came to me? Because you think this flannel shirt means I work here?"

He nodded frantically.

"I'll bet you're excited about all those presents you'll get under that tree. That's why you want it, right?"

He smiled wide. "Yes, sir."

"Yeah, I figured. But let me tell you a secret." I crooked my finger for him to come closer, and when his ear was by my mouth, I said, "Santa isn't real; it's just your mom's way of keeping your ass in line all year. So, no, I won't cut down a tree for all your fake presents, and no, I don't work here. Now get lost."

As the kid ran off crying, I dusted the snow off my shoulder and looked back at where Micah and his gentleman friend stood—only they were no longer there. The snot-nosed little brat had stolen my attention away from the only interesting thing that had happened since I arrived.

Ugh. Where the hell was that spiked cider?

MICAH

TREE FARM NIGHTS were my favorites of the year, no doubt about that. My siblings and I worked hard to make sure the people in our town felt like they were getting a special event, one they and their kids could look forward to every Christmas.

I was still grinning as I stomped the snow off my boots and brushed off the remnants of the snowman competition all over my jacket. How could anyone be unhappy on a night like this?

As I stepped inside the cabin and caught sight of Max vigorously rubbing his hands together by the fire, I had my answer.

I'd hoped that having him see the magic of the town coming together would invoke some sort of holiday spirit, but maybe he was too far gone in the cynical city mindset to care now. And if that were the case, I had to prepare myself for a miserable few days and a backfired plan.

Then again, maybe I underestimated him and he'd had a blast tonight.

"Stupid fucking snowballs," he muttered.

Okay, maybe not.

I hung my jacket, gloves, and scarf on a rack by the door and headed toward the couch, where Snoopy had taken up residence across the whole thing. I lifted his head to sit down and let him snuggle into my lap. "Snowballs, huh? Get caught up in a fight?"

"Not by choice. It would've been nice to get a heads-up before throwing one at my face."

"That wasn't enough heads-up for you?"

Max shot me a glare over his shoulder and continued to rub his fingers. "How long does it take for the blood to come back into your hands when you have frostbite?"

"Well, if it's frostbite, they're dead. We'll have to cut 'em off."

"You what?"

"Yeah, it's not pretty. Want me to get my saw from out back?" Panic flashed in Max's eyes, and it was so pure I found myself getting up off the couch to join him in front of the fire. "I'm sure it's not that dire, but let me see."

"Forget it."

"I *said*, let me see." I held my hand out, and when he gingerly placed one of his into my palm, I closed my fingers around it. The warmth from the fire had taken the bite of cold from his hand, but I gently squeezed and began to rub my thumb across the backs of his knuckles.

Max licked his lips, his eyes falling to the move, as we crouched there by the fire in an unusual moment of silence. The crackling of the flames sizzled and spat off the wood as I gestured for his other hand, and this time he complied without argument.

After a couple minutes of the same treatment, I looked up to see him watching me with narrowed eyes.

"Doesn't that feel better?"

Max, being Max, shrugged and pulled his hands free, then he straightened to his full height. "Wouldn't be necessary if I hadn't had to spend the night ho-ho-hoing with a bunch of merry maniacs. Honestly, who in their right mind wants to risk frostbite just so they can buy a blasted tree? They have stores for that."

I scoffed and shook my head. "And here I thought being around tonight's festivities might've cheered you up."

Max moved Snoopy's feet off a corner of the seat and flopped down on the couch, aiming a haughty eyebrow my way. "And how would they have done that? I almost got mowed down by a sled, I got snow in my boots *and* down my shirt, and then I had to watch you re-enact some sugary holiday romance that just made me feel sorry for the poor bastard you were brushing off. Good to know I'm not the only person you like stomping all over."

I narrowed my eyes as I got to my feet, my mind zeroing in on that last insult. "Sugary holiday romance?"

"I mean, really, the guy practically had hearts in his eyes as he smiled up at you, and you just smashed them all to pieces."

Wow, Max couldn't have been more wrong. But okay, if he wanted to go down this path, I was willing to see where his deluded mind would take him. "Oh, is that what I did?"

"Um, yes. The whole exchange was somewhat pathetic. Poor guy was all dressed up to see you. But you, being you, obviously didn't appreciate that, as you poured him his cider and sent him on his way. Really, Micah, you should learn to read a room."

I nodded. "You've got it all figured out, don't you?" I made my way back to the opposite end of the couch and lifted Snoopy's head up to take my place again, then angled myself so I was looking over the lazy mutt to Max. "Pity you're one hundred percent wrong. Good guess, though."

"I'm rarely wrong, but I'll humor you. How'd it go down, then? Don't bother telling me you didn't date, because I could see you did clear as day."

"I wouldn't lie. Edward was a big part of my past, but we each made our own decisions, and..." I shrugged and scratched the spot behind Snoopy's ear. "That's life."

"'That's life'? Really? That's all you have to say about it?"

"You want the whole tragic tale?"

"Couldn't have been too tragic if he still has hearts in his eyes."

There weren't hearts in his eyes, not at all, just a familiarity that came with seeing someone who used to be an important part of your life.

"Well, the long and short of it is he got a big opportunity in the city and decided to go for it."

"Ah, this explains a lot."

"It does?"

Max turned on the couch until he was facing me. "Sure it does. From the second I came up your drive, you've had it out for me, and now I know why. You have a hatred for all things city."

I cocked my head to the side, letting my eyes trail over him. "You really have no self-awareness, do you?"

"Actually, I think I possess plenty of self-awareness. I know exactly who I am and what I want out of life."

"Oh, I'd agree on that last statement for sure. But when it comes to *who* you are, that's where you're lacking."

Max rolled his eyes. "I know I'm going to regret this, but since it's either talk to you or go and hole up in a room the size of a coffin, I'll bite. What am I not seeing about myself?"

"What you represent."

"Class and sophistication?"

"Hardly. You see, you think my problem with you is that you're a city boy like Edward, and while some of that is true, my main problem is what you, as a person, have decided to represent."

Max scoffed but turned back to face the fire. "Oh, I can't wait to hear what you think that is."

"See, that right there is the first problem. You don't know when to stop talking—"

"That's not true."

I raised a brow, and he scowled at me. "You don't know when to stop talking and when to start listening. I must've told you in a hundred different ways that I am not interested in selling to you and your company, but you decided that wasn't going to work for you. You decided I didn't know my own mind and that your way was the best way. Even now, after a night like we just had with the town enjoying the holiday festivities, all you can do is sit here and complain about how they are all delusional and faking their enjoyment."

"And you think I'm wrong? Yeah, okay, people just *love* freezing their asses off for a few sleigh rides."

I patted Snoopy's head and shrugged. "I think the real person 'faking it' is you. You've forgotten how to enjoy yourself, so it's easier to act miserable. You're so caught up in the hustle and bustle of that city of yours that you have no idea what it means to stop and enjoy the life that's going on around you, and that's just sad."

Silence fell in the room until all that could be heard was the crackling of the fire as Max stared at the flames flickering in the hearth, and I felt a sudden pang of guilt. Maybe I'd been too harsh in my assessment, but damn, the guy had this ability to make my blood boil.

I was about to offer up some kind of apology when I heard, "It's not my fault. The city makes you that way."

Max tilted his head in my direction, and the light from the fire made the sharp angles of his handsome face even more distinct.

"From Thanksgiving on, that place is inundated with tourists rushing around the city like it's some kind of magical wonderland with no regard for those of us who still have to live and work there. It's ridiculous. The Christmas tree at Rockefeller, the parades, the stores all decking out their window fronts. What do you think they do that for? I tell you what, the money. So all those tourists and shop owners are no different to me. It's got nothing to do with magic or holiday spirit. For one month out of the year the world decides it's time to be nice to each other and spread joy and happiness, and it's all a big money grab."

Wow. I didn't really know what to say that. I didn't

think I'd ever met someone so against the holidays, and something about that made my heart ache for Max.

"You can't really believe that. What about your own family? You never spent time decorating the house and tree, and singing all the silly songs?"

"I don't want to talk about this anymore." Max got to his feet so abruptly that Snoopy whipped his head around to see what the commotion was all about. "It's been a long night. I'm going to bed."

I frowned at the sudden withdrawal. Max was usually at the ready with an argument or some kind of caustic comment on his tongue, but for the first time since I'd met him, he seemed...defeated. There was something more to this story I was missing, something to do with his family, but he'd shut down, that much was clear, and I didn't know him well enough to pry.

As he headed toward the stairs, I turned on the couch and called out his name. He stopped and looked back at me, and I decided to extend an olive branch.

"You ever been to a barn dance?"

Max's brows pulled into a deep V, and I laughed.

"I'm going to take that as a no."

"I hadn't even been *in* a barn until tonight."

I smirked at his answer. Scrooge was back. "Well, aren't you lucky—tomorrow is your chance to make it two nights in a row."

"You're asking me to a *barn* dance?"

I chuckled. "I guess I am. So rest up those frozen toes, frosty. I expect you to be rockin' around the Christmas tree with me tomorrow night."

Max groaned and rolled his eyes at my lame joke, and I

couldn't help but laugh as he trudged off up the stairs. Oddly enough, I was relieved his old Scroogy self was back, and I had to admit I was kind of looking forward to making him suffer. If there was one thing I would love to watch, it was Mr. Bah Humbug himself two-stepping along with the rest of Merrihill. Which meant I needed to ensure tomorrow night would go differently than it had today.

As the wheels began to turn, I stretched my legs out beneath Snoopy and watched the flames flicker and spark until my eyes turned heavy and the world went quiet.

MAXWELL

A HEAVY BANGING on the bedroom door the next morning jolted me up out of a deep sleep, and as I rubbed my eyes I realized I wasn't in the plush, comfy bed of clouds I'd been dreaming about, but tangled up in a quilt that didn't belong to me.

I groaned as the ache in my back reminded me of exactly where I was. As did the voice calling out from the hallway.

"Time to wake up, Scrooge—we've got a big day planned."

We? No. *We* did not have anything planned. The infuriating morning person waking me up at an hour that should be a crime did.

Before I could tell him I didn't plan on shoveling snow or lugging around decorations today, the door burst open and Micah's broad frame filled the entry. With the light streaming in behind him, I guessed it wasn't quite as early as I'd thought, but with someone who looked the way

Micah did, that wasn't exactly what I was paying attention to.

Okay, so maybe I wasn't a huge fan of flannel usually, but something about the way he wore it made it kinda... hot. It wasn't overly baggy like it was on me, but stretched across his muscles in a way that accentuated his body, and don't even get me started on the dark jeans his ass filled out to perfection. Not that I could see it right now, but once he turned around I knew exactly what view I'd get—and that may or may not have been from my staring at him every chance I got.

So Micah Noble was eye candy. So what? It didn't mean anything other than my time here wouldn't be completely without its perks.

Micah's gaze dropped to my hips, and his eyes widened slightly before a flush stained his cheeks and he looked away.

"Sorry, you might, uh, want to cover up."

I looked down to where the quilt had wrapped around one of my legs, leaving my naked body—yes, I'd decided to sleep naked last night—bare for Micah's perusal, but that wouldn't have been so bad if my stiff cock hadn't decided to be up and at 'em already.

"Well, what do you expect when you barge into someone's room?" I said, tugging the quilt across my lap.

"I expected the person who's been complaining about the cold to have a few more clothes on to keep warm."

"And here I thought I was too uptight to sleep naked." I yawned and covered it up with the back of my hand. "What's the rush? Someone decapitate a snowman?"

"I've got a couple errands to run and thought you might want to join me in a trip to town."

"And why would I do that?"

"To see the place you're so adamant to buy." He shrugged. "Or maybe to eat a hot breakfast instead of the oatmeal I have in my pantry. Either way."

Back home breakfast usually consisted of a few espresso shots on the way to the office, but I couldn't deny the thought of eggs and bacon sounded heavenly right about now.

"Okay, fine, you've convinced me," I said, throwing off the quilt and causing Micah to avert his eyes again. "I'll be ready in five."

IT WAS MORE like fifteen minutes later when we hopped into his truck, but hey, that was still a record for me and my unruly hair. It took a lot to tame down that mess, and Micah wasn't exactly rolling in hair products, apart from some gel that looked years old and not something he'd ever use.

Though it *did* look like something his ex would've used. He was put together, with the type of hair that would need to be slicked back, unlike Micah's. Had they lived together? Or had he just left it here on an overnight visit? Either way, both thoughts gnawed at me for some reason, but when Micah started the truck and Christmas tunes began to blare out of the speakers, it quickly left my head.

"You're really all in on this holiday stuff, huh?" I said over the music, and Micah only smiled softly as he drove down the plowed drive of his house. He must've gotten up early to do that. Would the rest of the roads into town be as lucky?

A few minutes into the drive, Micah smirked and turned the music down a smidge. "You're white-knuckling it pretty hard over there."

"Just hoping we don't go sliding off the road. I'm too young and handsome to die. Especially not here."

"No? You might get lucky and have a road named in your honor."

"Funny what each of us considers lucky. Sounds more like a nightmare to me."

Micah shook his head, but he was grinning. "In that case, you can stop stressing. I've got snow tires on this thing."

It was something of a relief to know we wouldn't be careening all over the place, and Micah was a better driver than I'd give him credit for out loud. No way would I give him *that* satisfaction.

"You better bust out your camera; we're entering downtown." Micah turned onto the super-originally named Main Street, and I prepared myself for the depressing sight of a one-lane road with empty buildings and snow piled up on sidewalks instead of people walking.

Imagine my surprise when downtown Merrihill wasn't anything like I expected.

I could only blink as we began to pass the shops on either side of us, the sidewalks clear and full of towns-people stopping every so often to say hello and chat. The buildings weren't vacant at all; in fact, they were rather unusual in that they had a European feel, each of them a different height, a different color, but all of them warm and welcoming, with icicle lights strung up along the edges of their tiled shingle roofs. It took me a minute to figure out what they reminded me of, and then it hit me—gingerbread houses.

"Nice, right?" Micah said as he pulled into a parking space and shut off the engine.

I picked my jaw up off the floor before facing him and trying for a nonchalant shrug. "It's okay."

Micah smirked. "Sure." Then he popped open his door, and I followed suit, my stomach more than ready for the promised hot breakfast. But instead of leading us into a restaurant to satiate my hunger, Micah walked toward one of the stores we'd parked near, one called Watson's Threads.

I took one look at the mannequins in the window and frowned. "Tell me this is just one of your errands."

"It is. For *you*."

"Uh, why?"

"I figured you'd want to look your best for a tour about town, and you've complained about my clothes long enough."

"Wait, you want me to buy clothes...here?" I gave one of the mannequins another once-over and wrinkled my nose. "But—"

"But nothing. You'll be here a few more days, and I'm sure you'd rather wear something that fits, am I right?"

I bit down on my lip, not wanting to agree but realizing I'd be stupid not to find a pair of pants that didn't drop off my hips without a belt. "Maybe."

"So would you rather waste time arguing about it out here, or can we go inside somewhere warm?"

"You know, you could be a charming guy if the essence of snark wasn't behind everything you say."

"I could say the same for you, Scrooge." Micah opened the door and waved me through. "After you."

As I entered the shop, the first thing I noticed was the scent of men's cologne mixed with something wintery, like balsam and spiced apples. It was the one appealing thing this place had going for it, because the style of clothing hanging from the racks was nothing I'd wear in real life.

"Welcome to Watson's Threads." An older man with rosy cheeks stepped out from the back, and when he caught sight of Micah, he gave us a bright smile. "Why, Micah Noble, Betty and I were just talking about you. Everything all set for the dance tonight?"

"You know it, Terry. I hope that means we'll see you there."

"We wouldn't miss it. One of our favorite nights of the whole year."

Micah shot me a meaningful look. "Happy to hear it. We've got a fancy city man to impress."

"That would be me," I said, pointing to myself. "The fancy city man."

"Oh." Terry looked me over, and a frown puzzled his forehead. "I wouldn't have guessed that. You seem to fit right in, don't ya?"

Uh, absolutely the hell *not*. Why would he even think that? "Me? Fit in...here? I don't think so."

"He means because of your clothes," Micah murmured before saying to Terry, "Max's car broke down up here and he got stranded for a few days. I let him borrow some of my clothes, but as you can see, they're a little big. Think you can help us out with something closer to his size?"

"It'd be my pleasure. Let's see..." Terry gave me another once-over and threw out a number, correctly guessing my size, and then he took off through the store with the energy of a man half his age.

"Nice, isn't he?" Micah said, giving me a nudge to follow after him.

"If you say so."

As Micah brought up the rear, I ran my hands over the racks of clothes we passed, surprised to find that although they weren't my style, the quality was topnotch. And yeah, maybe this Terry guy was nice too, but I couldn't admit any of that to Micah.

To him, everything and everyone had to be horrible from an outsider's perspective, or none of this was going to work. If I told him I thought downtown looked kinda cute or that the people were friendly, he would never leave. The whole point of my being here was to get Micah to take that big, dangling carrot I was offering and get the hell out.

Being anything less than the Scrooge he called me was counterintuitive to the plan.

"Not exactly the designer brands I was hoping for," I said loudly. "Is there anything in this store that won't make me look like a lumberjack?"

A stern push and low *"Shut up"* from behind only had me feeling more emboldened.

Terry motioned to one of the mannequins in the corner of the room, dressed in a simple pair of khaki pants and a black sweater and surrounded by Christmas lights. "What do you think of something like that?"

I couldn't help it. Business-minded Maxwell had taken over, and I couldn't stop the words from coming out of my mouth. "It's nice...but it's not really my style. Do you have anything that's a little more, I don't know, tailored? A little less khaki?"

Terry glanced behind me at Micah before meeting my eyes again. "I'm sure I can accommodate you. Why don't we look at something more like this?" He pulled a collared shirt from the rack, along with a pair of black pants. "I'm sure this is much more up your alley, and it would look wonderful on you. We had this shipped in from Rochester; just got here yesterday."

Not bad. Not bad at all. But still not exactly my style. "It's better, but I can't really see myself wearing it anywhere other than here. It's still a little...country for my tastes." I sauntered down the aisle, tapping each hanger as I went. "Nope, nope, none of this will work. Do you have anything in cashmere? This mix blend of the cheaper materials irritates my skin."

"Max, come on," Micah said. "Surely you can find something in here."

"Eh, I don't think so."

Terry placed the shirt on the rack and slowly backed away. "I'm going to give you two a minute to...discuss. I'll be over there when you're ready."

The man practically ran off, and as soon as he was out of earshot, Micah was in my face.

"Are you really trying to tell me you can't find anything in here? Or are you being difficult on purpose?"

"I was telling the truth. Mixed blends *do* irritate my skin."

Micah pinched the bridge of his nose like he was trying for patience. "Okay, listen, this is the only place in town you're going to find something that fits you. So unless you want to keep walking around looking like a potato sack, Terry is it. He's also a good person who didn't deserve your being a brat."

"Calm down, it's not like he owns the place."

"Actually, genius, he does."

At Micah's revelation my stomach dropped, followed by the smug-ass smirk I still wore.

"Terry's the owner? But I thought..."

"You thought what?"

I sputtered in response because...well, I was such an ass.

"I get you're annoyed you're stuck out here in the middle of nowhere, but can't you try to take in the moment? Maybe see it as a good thing, a moment to—"

"If you say 'find myself,' I might gag."

"I was going to *say*, a moment to rediscover the magic of being unplugged. Of slowing down and appreciating what's around you?" I glanced around the store, and Micah held up a finger to my lips. "Unless what you're about to say is nice, don't say it."

I sighed and rolled my eyes. "Okay, you're right. I guess I need to lighten up a bit. I'm sure if I dig through these racks I'll find something."

"Now there's the spirit." Micah clapped me on the shoulder. "And you're also going to apologize to Terry."

My mouth fell open, a refusal at the ready, but the stubborn expression on Micah's face told me that I was not going to be able to talk myself out of that.

"Fine, I'll apologize. I realize my tongue can get away from me at times, and I really wasn't trying to be insulting."

Micah smirked. "You know, somehow I believe that. I think it's just a talent of yours."

"You can leave now." The last thing I needed was Micah standing by monitoring my groveling expertise, because let's be real, he'd no doubt find them lacking.

"Oh, I'm not going anywhere. But you are. Terry's waiting on you."

I narrowed my eyes as Micah crossed his arms and stood his ground, then I turned and headed toward the back, weaving through the aisles until Terry's back came into view behind the counter.

Don't coward out now. "Excuse me, Terry?"

The man hesitated before turning around, and though he forced a closed smile on his face, I could see the hurt lurking in his eyes.

I was a shit. And I figured I should probably tell him so.

"I'm an asshole," I blurted.

Whatever Terry had been expecting me to say, it wasn't that, because his mouth parted and he said, "I beg your pardon?"

"Micah called me a fancy city boy when we walked in, but that was just him being nice. I'm actually an asshole, and I never should've said what I did about your clothes. It wasn't true." I ran my hand through my unruly hair and sighed. "It's really not about your store. Or you. I just wanted to hate on this place because it affects my bottom line. Which I know makes no sense to you, other than to make me sound even more terrible, but...just know I'm incredibly sorry for what I said."

"Apology accepted."

Oh. Just like that? I expected to have to grovel more.

"I hope you can find something to appreciate in town before you go. Take care, Max." As Terry began to turn away, I found that the guilt still swishing around in my gut hadn't been eased with such a quick acceptance. There had to be some way to make it up to him that would let him know I meant it.

"Wait, just one more thing," I said. "I'd, uh...like to buy two of everything." The words came flying out of my mouth before I even realized what I was saying.

That caught his attention. "You'd like what?"

Shit, no backtracking now. "Two of everything in the store."

"Max, that's really not necessary—"

"Sir, I'd be honored to wear your clothes, and I'm sure someone else would enjoy them as well, so...two of all of it. Shirts, pants, ties, accessories, ring it all up."

I had a feeling Terry wasn't left speechless often, but his mouth moved in a way that looked like he was trying to find words and failing. It took a long minute before he said, "That might take a while."

"I've got a while. As a matter of fact, Micah mentioned breakfast, so if I can get something to wear while I'm out, I can pick up the rest later."

A smile slowly spread across Terry's face. "Are you sure?"

"Absolutely positive." I fished my credit card out of my

wallet and handed it over. "Just charge everything to my card and we can swing back by later."

Terry stared down at the card in disbelief, shaking his head, and then pointed at the rack beside me. "Why don't we get you started with those, and I'll grab Eli from the back to get the rest going. And if we're not finished by the time you come back, I can always bring them by before the dance."

"I appreciate that. And I'm sorry again for...well, all of it."

As I turned to grab one of the shirts closest to me to go put on, I ran straight into Micah, face-planting into his broad chest.

How long had he been standing there? Had he heard my apology, or was he coming to check on his friend? I got my answer when I looked up at his face, but this time there was no disappointment in his eyes, only admiration and awe, as I walked past him toward the front door and called out over my shoulder, "By the way, you're buying breakfast, because I just spent all my money."

MICAH

TO SAY I was shocked by what Max had just done at Watson's Threads would be an understatement. His initial disdain for the local clothing options had brought out the protective side of me, but I hadn't meant to guilt him into buying practically the entire store.

Oh well, if he could afford it, I wasn't going to stop him, and Terry had practically passed out upon hearing the offer, even agreeing to drive the purchases out to my place later this evening so he wouldn't have to rush bagging it all up now.

It was strange, the dichotomy between the façade Max put on and the person I could see peeking out every now and then, and his interaction with Terry had been a perfect example. It made me curious about which side of him was the real one, because there was no denying that the more vulnerable, kind side of him was seriously attractive, though I did appreciate the fun snark a bit too. Not that I'd tell him that.

"So, you hungry now, or did you want to grab something later?" I asked as we wandered down Main Street. Max had been uncharacteristically quiet since leaving the store, but for the first time since we'd met, it didn't feel uncomfortable.

"What? You mean you didn't hear my stomach growling back there?"

"No, I was too busy listening to you run your mouth. But if you were that hungry, we could've eaten before we shopped."

"Are you kidding?" Max looked appalled. "No one tries on clothes *after* they eat."

"They don't?"

"No. You want to see new clothes for the first time when you look and feel amazing."

I stopped on the snow-covered sidewalk and looked down at him, a frown forming between my brows. "And you feel amazing when you're hungry?"

Max started to laugh. "Well, no, but I look better than after I've wolfed down a meal the size of Texas."

I eyed him from head to toe, not believing for a second that he could eat anything other than the polite portions of a fine dining restaurant.

"What?" he asked when he noticed my perusal.

"Nothing." I shook my head and then started up the street again.

Max jogged to catch up. "That was not a nothing look. What'd I do now? Let me guess, you have relatives in Texas and I somehow just offended all of them."

I chuckled and glanced at him, and the glint in his eyes

told me he was also enjoying this new kind of ease we'd slipped into.

"I don't have any relatives in Texas, and even if I did, nothing about what you just said was offensive."

As we arrived at the small diner, I held open the door, and as he went to walk by, he stopped. "Then what was the look about?"

"Did it ever occur to you that I was looking at you for a *good* reason?"

Max narrowed his eyes. "Like what?"

I once again trailed my eyes down over his new clothes. "Like...I like what I see."

Max scoffed and shook his head. "Yeah, okay. Because a sweater is so becoming."

It was, actually. These new clothes—that actually fit him—had taken the city out of the Scrooge who'd arrived and given him a more relaxed, easygoing vibe that was much more approachable and...sexy.

"Sweaters are cozy," I said as I gestured for him to move inside.

"*Cozy?* Now there's a hell of a compliment. You basically just made me sound like a blanket."

I laughed as I pointed out a window booth for us to sit in. Kathy's Diner was your typical American diner, with old blue vinyl-covered seats and white laminated tabletops, and on each of those tables were plastic-covered menus that every local knew by heart.

"I was giving you a compliment," I said.

Max slid into the booth, and I did the same, and when our knees bumped under the table, I noticed him swallow and shift on his seat.

"Sorry." I picked up one of the menus and held it out to him. "Long legs. I can't really move them anywhere else."

Max's cheeks flushed as he picked up the menu, and when he began to read it intently, I couldn't help but take a second to admire the view.

Maxwell Scott was an incredibly attractive guy. With his usually perfect hair a little windswept from the weather, and his lips redder than usual, his features were more enhanced today, and when you added in the spots of color now highlighting his cheeks, I had to shift on my seat.

Max looked up as my leg grazed his, and when our eyes caught, I felt something shift in the air. From the moment he'd showed up at my house there'd been this tension between us, this clash of wills over why he was there. But right now, in this moment, it felt different. This felt more like a...date.

Hang on a second. A date?

"Okay, you're the local, so what's good here?"

I blinked and shoved my thoughts aside, and instead focused on the question at hand. *What's good here?* "Everything."

Max cocked his head to the side. "Everything, really? Geez, Micah, that's super helpful."

"Geez, Max, it's the truth. It's not my fault you're indecisive."

"I'm not indecisive; there's just a *lot* to choose from here." His eyes fell back to the menu. "What do you like?"

"Hmm—"

"If you say everything again, I swear I will kick you."

I grinned at his threat of bodily harm and then leaned across the table. "Go ahead, I dare you."

Something in my voice must've reminded him that the likelihood of his coming out the victor in anything physical with me was highly unlikely. So instead, he went back to staring at his many options.

"Look, if you really can't decide, leave it with me and I'll order for you."

Max's eyes widened, his horror over that idea clear as day.

"What, you don't trust me?"

"No, it's just, that's very, um...you know..."

"Nice of me?"

"No. I mean, it is, but that's not what I'm getting at."

"Well, if you want to eat sometime this century, could you maybe fill me in?"

"I just mean that that's a very *relationship* kind of thing, isn't it?" He looked around at the other customers and waitstaff. "I wouldn't want people here to get the, uh, wrong idea. You know, this being a small town and all."

"And you know a lot about this? Being in a relationship?"

"Actually, I don't know anything at all. I don't date."

"*Ever?*"

"Ever."

"Wow..." I wasn't sure why I was all that surprised—I knew the guy was a workaholic. I just figured with a face like his, Max would have plenty of men lining up to take him out. As long as they knew about his penchant for trying to buy out people's dreams and smashing them to smithereens, of course. "Too busy or not interested?"

"Hmm, never been interested enough to not be busy. That makes sense?"

"Yep, sure does. Hey, whatever works for you. Personally, I'd get lonely."

Max looked skeptical. "Really? You live all the way out in the middle of nowhere. I wouldn't think companionship was high on your list of priorities."

"Then you'd think wrong. I love having someone around to share the fire."

"And help cut the wood?"

I couldn't help my laugh. "Comes in handy."

"Mhmm. I figured, but let's not start up the gossip mill over something that's not true. You order yours and I'll order mine. I'm sure I can decide on something here."

I leaned back in the booth and crossed my arms, and couldn't help but notice the way Max's eyes roved down over me.

I liked that. I liked that *a lot*.

"So let me get this straight, you'd rather sit there and go hungry than have me order for you on the off chance someone here might think we're on a date?"

And that *was* exactly what they were all thinking. I wasn't delusional.

Max shrugged but nodded. "Yeah, I just don't want you to be uncomfortable, that's all."

"Oh, okay." I smirked and gestured to Kathy that we were ready to order. "Well, thank you for looking out for *my* golden-boy reputation. It's much appreciated."

My sarcasm landed with the exact amount of punch I wanted, judging by the scowl that crossed Max's face. But just as he was about to fire off something caustic in return, Kathy stopped by our table and flashed her most welcoming smile.

"Micah, it's so lovely to see you in here this morning. I can't tell you how much fun the family and I had last night out at the tree farm."

"That's great to hear, Kathy. You and the rugrats are some of my toughest critics, so it's always nice to know I've impressed you."

"Oh, stop." She placed a friendly hand on my shoulder and squeezed. "You never disappoint. The Nobles never do."

"Thanks for that." I patted her hand. "I'll let them all know. Or *you* can tonight. You are coming to the dance, right?"

"You bet we are. I already picked out a dress, and George is getting off early to take me."

"Ah, good man."

"Don't I know it." She turned to the unfamiliar face at the table and grinned. "Now, who might you be?"

"I'm Maxwell—"

"You can call him Max," I interrupted, earning a glare from Scrooge.

"I'm staying out at the Noble farm for a couple of days."

"Oh, how nice. Have you ever been there before?" Kathy asked.

"No, this, um, this is my first time."

"And what a perfect time of the year for it. The town loves the Nobles' Christmas tree farm; it's just such a special place. The heart and soul of Merrihill. It's magical."

Max looked across the table at me, and I couldn't help my smug grin, because hadn't I been telling him that all along?

"That's what I keep hearing."

"Well, if last night didn't convince you, then the dance will." She held her notepad to her heart and sighed, closing her eyes. "It's one of the most romantic nights of the year."

It really is, I mouthed, and Max's cheeks flushed even brighter. Hmm... I was really starting to like this shier, almost demure side of him. It was endearing and really damn hot.

"Well, I digress," Kathy said. "You two don't want me hanging around all morning. What can I get for you?"

She looked to Max first, waiting on his answer, but then he gestured to me with a soft smile I'd never seen before—a smile I knew I'd never forget.

"Micah's going to order for me."

"Oh is he now?" She turned to me, a suggestive twinkle in her eye. "What can I get for you and your beau over here?"

And there it was, the immediate assumption that this was a date. I chuckled and didn't even bother correcting her. There was no point. She'd believe what she wanted to. And also... I kind of liked it.

"We'll have the steak and eggs, pancake stack, and side of bacon, please."

Max's eyes bugged. "Each?"

"You said you could wolf down a plate the size of Texas."

"It was just a metaphor."

"Well, now you can give it a real Texas try."

"Sooo, we good?" Kathy asked, looking between the two of us.

I nodded. "We're good."

"You got it." She picked up the menus and tucked them under her arm. "Anything to drink?"

I knew from his time at my house Max was a coffee drinker. "Two coffees and some OJ, please."

"No problem. I'll have it out ASAP."

"Thanks, Kathy."

As she walked off, Max leaned over the table and whispered, "She totally thinks we're on a date."

I sat forward until only inches separated our faces, and this time tangled my legs with his on purpose.

"Hmm, I don't know if I'd call this a date, but I guess that all depends now, doesn't it?"

"On?"

"On how it ends." My attention shifted to his mouth, and in that moment I knew exactly how I wanted this to end. My lips, on his.

I raised my eyes back to Max's, and I could swear I saw the same flicker of heat I was feeling swirl in those dark depths.

"About the dance tonight..." I sat back in my seat, as did Max, and after a moment of silence, he cleared his throat.

"Yeah?"

"You still up for going with me?"

That soft, shy smile from earlier hit Max's lips again. "As in an actual...date?"

"Yeah. One where we both forget why you're here and just enjoy the moment."

"Are you trying to romance me, Mr. Noble?"

"Maybe."

"By dancing in a *barn*?"

"You're missing the point, Scrooge. The romance isn't about dancing in a barn. It's about *who* you're dancing with in the barn." I winked at him, more than willing to accept this challenge. "And you're dancing with me. So get ready to be swept off your feet."

TRUE TO HIS word, Terry had dropped off package after package, filling Micah's small space with so many clothes that I wasn't sure how I'd manage to get them upstairs. So while Micah had joined his family in getting things ready at the barn, I rummaged through the clothes to find something suitable to wear. Apparently jeans wouldn't do at this particular event, which was surprising to me, considering the venue, but after too many hours in casual attire, I was more than ready to look like my usual self again. Or as close to it as I could get. I had no idea what Micah had done with the suit I'd come here in, but then, maybe that would be *too* much for a night like tonight.

A dance...in a barn. That wasn't something that would usually be up my alley, but I couldn't stop thinking about what Micah had said earlier. *You're dancing with me. So get ready to be swept off your feet.*

Damn, I'd never really been attracted to the tall,

hulking lumberjack type before, but this forced time and proximity with Micah was making me see and feel things I never had before. Like earlier today after breakfast, when he'd insisted on showing me around his little town. I'd expected to feel put out by the notion, eager to get back to his place and dive back into all of the reasons he should sell his property to me. But the more time he'd spent walking me around the snow-covered sidewalks and in and out of the little boutique shops, the more charmed I became. Merrihill was more than just some little backward town in the middle of nowhere—it was an experience unlike any I'd had before. Quaint, charming, and full of Christmas joy. The fact it could charm me and my jaded heart had to mean something, right?

Or maybe it's the company I'm keeping...

I walked over to the small window in my room and looked out at the farm below. Micah and his siblings were outside buzzing around the place getting it ready for tonight's dance, and I had to admit, I was happy to be inside as opposed to out there.

The snow had started falling on our drive home from town, and as I stared down at the Nobles shoveling the path up to the barn for the umpteenth time, I couldn't help but wonder what poor bastard was going to be on shovel duty tonight.

I scanned the property, searching out the man that I couldn't seem to get out of my head, and when I spotted Micah standing on a ladder by the barn door hanging a string of lights, my heart began to thump a little harder.

This was crazy. I didn't even know the guy, and let's be real, we hadn't exactly been on the best terms since I accidentally stranded myself at his house. But between his offering me a place to stay despite my wanting to acquire his land, and today in town when he'd agreed to take me on a date, my fool heart was acting like a jackhammer every time I looked at him.

I sighed and stepped away from the window. The last thing I needed was for him to see me mooning over him like some lovesick princess locked in her tower. So instead, I went back to deciding what to wear.

A pair of black slacks was a given, and I quickly threw those on and debated between a couple of shirts, finally deciding on a crisp maroon button-down.

All right, let's see what I'm working with, I thought as I headed toward the bathroom mirror. It'd taken the better part of a half-hour to tame the waves that this weather seemed to inspire, but as I looked at myself, I realized maybe they didn't look so bad after all. I was just used to smoothing everything down: my hair, my clothes, hell, even my personality. Of course Micah brought out the feisty side of me, but that had been half the fun so far, hadn't it?

With a critical eye, I unbuttoned, rebuttoned, then unbuttoned again the collar of the shirt before deciding to leave it open. *Okay, this isn't so bad.* I'd fully expected the clothes to look and fit a little on the cheap side, but they actually felt good and looked even better.

Damn. Maybe I was just a snob.

"Maaax!" a woman's voice yelled from downstairs, and I stuck my head into the hallway to see who it was. Gina stood in the front entrance, door open wide and letting all the cold air in. "The dance is starting now. Micah said get your ass to the barn."

I smirked. "Were those his exact words?"

"Close enough. Come on."

Before I could tell her I was coming, she was out the door, slamming it shut behind her. For some reason in that moment, I felt a flutter of nerves in my stomach and wondered what that meant.

Not wanting to dwell on it, I gave myself a final look and then made my way downstairs, stopping by the door to throw on one of my new coats before heading outside.

Just like last night, I could hear the music and chatter of excited voices from a distance, and as the barn came into view, I watched the line of people head inside and made my way down to join them.

Amazing how a whole town came together for a barn dance. And for the tree farm events. Almost like they took pride in where they lived and wanted to support each other. Would that still be the case if a resort took up residence in this spot?

And why was I now thinking *if* instead of *when?*

Don't think about that tonight, I told myself as I followed the crowd into the barn. The last thing I needed was to think about work, especially when I knew a gorgeous man was on the other side of the wall waiting for me.

My stomach did that whole tingling, flippy thing again, and I had to take a deep breath of the cold night air to shock it into submission. When had I started thinking of Micah as a gorgeous man and not man-I-need-for-work-purposes-only? Not that I hadn't always thought he was attractive—I mean, what was hotter than a man with muscles filling out a pair of jeans and wielding an ax? Not much.

"Look how beautiful it is," the woman in front of me said as we entered the barn, and as the full scope of it came into view, I had to agree. Last night the interior was bright and open, but tonight it had been transformed into a dimmer, more intimately lit space, with twinkling lights and fresh garlands strung up around the room. There were several tables on one side for anyone taking a rest from the dance floor, but the majority of couples were already up swaying to Elvis's "Blue Christmas."

I did a quick scan, hoping I wouldn't see Micah out there with someone else, but when there were no six-five heads poking up out of the crowd, I let myself breathe a sigh of relief.

Why was I stressing about that, anyway? He'd invited me here. He said I'd be dancing with him, that he would be sweeping me off my feet, which I didn't think had ever happened to me in my lifetime, but I was up for the challenge.

But first—I needed a drink.

Someone I didn't recognize was manning the bar, and there was more than just hot chocolate on the menu tonight.

"Hey there," the bartender said, smiling brightly, as everyone in this town seemed to do. "Can I interest you in mulled cider or one of our special candy cane cocktails?"

"You wouldn't happen to have a shot of whiskey hiding behind there, would you?"

"Sorry, no, but I can throw in an extra shot of peppermint vodka in the cocktail."

I cringed at the thought and shook my head. "Let's go with the cider."

"Coming right up."

For a premade drink, it was surprisingly good, nice and strong, and it warmed my body in a way that had me shaking off my coat.

"Is that Maxwell Scott taking his clothes off in the middle of a crowded room?" Micah's deep voice behind me had me turning around, and damn. Maybe it was the drink going to my head already, but the man smirking down at me looked good enough to eat.

Okay, maybe don't think that *in a crowded room.*

"May I?" Micah didn't wait for my answer before taking my coat and laying it over a nearby chair. Wow, color me shocked—chivalry still existed. "I wasn't sure if you'd voluntarily make an appearance tonight or if I'd have to come looking for you."

"You promised me a date, did you not?"

"I did."

I looked around at all the lights and glitter and then back to the gorgeous man in front of me and took a step closer. "You also promised to sweep me off my feet."

Micah's eyes all but twinkled under the lights as he held his hand out and nodded. "So I did."

I placed my hand in his, and when our fingers touched, it was like coming into contact with a live wire. A jolt of electricity sizzled up my arm, and when Micah tugged me forward, my feet automatically went.

"Do you have a favorite song?"

I couldn't help my grin, because I had a feeling I knew where he was going with this. "Why? Have you got a special 'in' with the DJ?"

"Maybe?"

I chuckled and looked around at all the smiling couples making their way around the dance floor to Elvis's bluesy tune, and had a sudden urge to join them out there with this man.

There was only one problem:

"I don't really know any Christmas songs. Just the overly cheery ones, and that doesn't really make me think of being swept off my—"

Micah's burst of laughter cut me off as he placed his finger up to my lips, then he let go of my hand and began to walk away from me. "I got this. You just wait here."

"Where else would I go?" I flashed a cheeky grin his way. "My car doesn't work, remember?"

Micah's feet faltered for a second, and I almost thought he was going to trip until he stopped and righted himself.

"Uneven floor," he muttered, and when I looked down to see perfectly aligned wood, I frowned. I was about to joke with him on how he planned to sweep me off his feet if he couldn't even stand on his, but before I could get the words out, he was gone.

I moved off to the side to watch the other couples as they whispered sweet nothings to one another and moved effortlessly around the dance floor, and thought that maybe I did have a skewed vision of this holiday.

Sure, I grew up in one of the biggest and brightest cities in the world, a place people came to celebrate this time of the year. But my family had always been so deeply rooted in the hustle and bustle of the business life there that they'd never taken a moment to just stop and enjoy it. Even when I was a kid, Christmas had always been more of an afterthought to my parents than a holiday to spend time with the family.

Don't forget to get money out for Maxwell's card this year, dear...

Yeah, there was nothing like hearing your parents discussing a trip to the ATM in lieu of what cookie to put out for Santa.

But that felt so far away right now. The buildings, the tourists, the hustle and bustle of it all. It felt so far removed from the here and now, and for the first time ever I was going to try to look at this through a different lens—Micah's lens.

"Did you miss me?"

I jumped at the deep voice by my ear and glanced over my shoulder. "You scared me. How'd you get over here without me seeing you? I swear, for a big guy you move with the stealth of a ninja."

Micah's lips quirked, and with his standing this close, I was almost tempted to lean in and see if they tasted as good as they looked.

"Out here, you have to be stealthy. Especially when it comes to huntin' season."

I raised a brow, leaning back from him a ways. "Huntin' season? Really? Are you just trying to trip me up now, turning all country?"

Micah chuckled. "No, I'm being serious. Something you should keep in mind around here. You never know who might be creeping up behind you."

"Okay, I thought you were going to romance me tonight. Not try to scare me half to death."

"No need to worry. If you hear anything rattling around

on the roof at night, it's more than likely a possum."

"And that's supposed to make me feel *better?*"

I shook my head, and when Micah held up another cup of cider, I quickly downed it in several gulps.

"Okay, well, I guess I was right in bringing that over."

"If you keep talking about wild animals trying to get in the house at night, I'm going to need several more of those."

Micah grinned, and when a familiar violin refrain began, Micah took my empty cup and placed it on one of the tables set up in the barn.

"Wait, I know this song..."

"I'd be disappointed if you didn't." Micah took my hand and led me out to the dance floor. "No one sings 'The Christmas Song' quite like Nat King Cole."

As his fingers engulfed mine, Micah took my waist, pulling me into his arms, and I placed a hand over his heart and stared up into his handsome face. "So is this your secret weapon?"

"Secret weapon?"

"In sweeping me off my feet."

"It's definitely part of it. I've always thought this song to be one of the most beautiful ever written for the season."

"Huh..."

Micah's lips crooked as he led us from one step to the next, and he was right—he really was good at this dancing business.

"What?" he said.

"Oh, nothing."

"You don't think I know when you're thinking something?" Micah brushed his thumb over the back of my knuckles. "Come on, out with it, city boy. What was that 'huh' all about?"

I opened my mouth, about to tell him, but then shut it as I thought over my words carefully.

Micah laughed, and his entire being lit up with pure joy. "It must be something *real* good if you're trying to work out how to say it nicely."

"No." I shook my head. "It's not bad. I just... I think you might be changing my opinion on this song, that's all."

"Oh?"

"Yeah. I'd thought that first night at the tree farm that no one in their right mind would want Jack Frost nipping at their nose."

"Ahh, I see." Micah deftly turned us in a well-executed spin, then leaned down to brush a kiss across the end of my nose. I sucked in a shocked breath, and he winked. "Maybe I can help change your mind."

The intensity in Micah's eyes as he stared down at me made my heart pound, along with other parts of my body. How had I gone from thinking this man utterly ridiculous to thinking he was absolutely wonderful?

But it was true: Micah Noble had somehow managed to chip away at my coal-black heart and make me see the wonder that was Christmas.

I started to laugh, and Micah grinned. "What?"

"I was just thinking that you already have changed my mind about Christmas."

Micah moved forward two steps, and I automatically backed up until we were off the main dance floor and swaying gently in the shadows.

I looked around and noticed he'd maneuvered us away from the rest of the dancers, and my pulse began to race.

"Trying to get me alone now, huh?"

"Maybe," Micah said, his voice low and raspy. He lowered his head and said by my ear, "Look up."

In truth, I didn't want to look at anything but him. But for some reason, I couldn't deny him.

I glanced up to see a sprig of mistletoe hanging haphazardly from a piece of string. "Did you just put that—"

Before I could finish my thought, my lips were taken by firm, full ones that were surrounded by a soft beard and sure of what they were doing. My stomach flipped and my breath caught as Micah let go of my waist and reached up to cradle my cheek.

A low moan escaped me as he flicked his tongue over my lower lip and then gently sucked on it, and I immediately opened for him. The hungry groan that filled my ears blocked out whatever song the DJ had switched to next as I slid my hand over Micah's shoulder and gripped the back of his neck.

Micah pushed his tongue between my lips and rubbed it up against mine, and I wasn't sure if it was him or the mulled cider, but my head spun. He tasted like a warm winter's night, and all I wanted to do was curl up in his lap and purr like a contented kitten.

After what felt like an eternity, Micah kissed along my jaw to my ear and whispered, "Why would you want something this magical to ever come to an end?"

Good question, and one I didn't have answer for right now. Because all I could think of as I reached for him again was: how could I make this moment last forever?

MICAH

I. COULDN'T. SLEEP.

It'd been hours since the last guest had packed up their dancing shoes. Hours since I'd turned out the lights and kicked all my siblings off the property. Hours since I'd held Max in my arms, and *hours* since I'd kissed him like I'd known him my entire life.

But as I lay in bed staring at my ceiling, sleep remained elusive. My mind rewound and replayed every single moment of that kiss in high definition. Max's shock, his sweetness, and his pliancy when he'd finally given in to the attraction that'd been swirling around us now for days. It'd been a moment unlike any I'd ever had before, and now that I'd had a sample, I wanted more.

I shifted under the covers, restless as I plumped my pillow up behind me, and Snoopy grumbled as we both settled back in and I closed my eyes, trying to banish the memories of the man sleeping one floor above.

I wasn't a fool. I knew this couldn't go anywhere. Max

and I were complete opposites. He was Mr. Corporate, a city boy, all the way down to his leather loafers, and no amount of twinkle lights and cider could change that—*or* the reason he was here in the first place. A reason I'd conveniently pushed aside so I wouldn't have to analyze my questionable choices, because what would the family think if they knew I wanted to go upstairs, strip down the man who wanted to destroy our property, and spend the next twelve hours destroying his body instead?

Exactly. *Questionable* didn't even begin to describe my misguided thoughts, and the best thing I could do for all of us now was to shut my eyes and go to sleep—so that was exactly what I did.

As my mind drifted off to the elusive land of dreams, the sound of floorboards creaking underfoot had my eyes flashing open and my ears listening closely. It was late, or really early morning depending on how you looked at it, and after the night's festivities, I thought for sure Max would be passed out.

Maybe something had happened to wake him. A possum on the roof? It could happen. Or was he cold? Did he need a drink? I had no idea, but as I shifted up to my elbow to listen to what direction he was headed, the wooden boards by my bedroom creaked a little louder.

Snoopy raised his sleepy head at the disturbance, but when the door remained shut, he promptly laid his head back on my feet, seemingly unconcerned with our safety. *Some guard dog you are,* I thought, about to get up and see what Max needed, when the handle twisted and the door pushed open an inch.

The light from the fireplace in the living room still

crackled down low and silhouetted Max's figure as he slipped inside my bedroom and then gently closed the door behind him.

He stood there for a moment with his back facing me, and when a few seconds passed and he said nothing, I lounged back against my pillow and asked, "You get lost or something, city boy?"

Max straightened, and when he turned to face me, the twinkling lights from outside made his eyes glow in the soft light.

Tonight at the dance I'd thought Max one of the most handsome men I'd ever seen. But as he stood there in my bedroom with his lounge pants resting low on his hips and a black tank stretched taut across his lean body, my thoughts turned to something much more heated.

"I'll have you know that even us city boys still have a pretty good sense of direction."

I couldn't argue that. It had led him right here, to my bedroom. "Is that right?"

"Mhmm." He nodded and pushed off the door, taking several steps closer to the king-sized sleigh bed that occupied most of my room, then shook his head. "Of course you have a massive bed."

"Of course I do."

My dick jerked under his watchful gaze, and as I stretched out beneath the covers, I was thankful for the heavy comforter over the top of my naked body, otherwise the conversation might be more focused on my massive—

"Tonight was fun."

I grinned at the idle chitchat, as though it were totally normal that Max had snuck into my room in the early hours of the morning to tell me he had a great time at a barn dance.

"It was. I especially liked the last part." *And want to do it all over again.*

"I liked that too."

"Oh yeah?"

Max bit down on his lower lip, the same lip I'd sucked on earlier during the hottest kiss of my life. "So much that I can't stop thinking about it."

"And that's why you're here now?"

Max lowered his eyes over me and nodded. "Part of it."

Damn, his lustful look was matching the desire in my dick. "What's the other part?"

"I want to do it again."

Oh shit, there goes my self-restraint. How was I supposed to ignore my feelings when he was voicing my exact thoughts out loud?

"Max?"

"Hmm?"

"If you don't mean what you're saying, now is the time to leave. Because I'm about to climb out of this bed and do exactly what you just asked."

Max swallowed but made no move to exit the room as I tossed the covers aside and moved to my feet. The second my naked body came into view, a soft groan filled the air. His eyes greedily took in every inch of skin that was on display, and as I wasn't exactly a small guy, that was a whole hell of a lot of skin. My cock was thick and hard, and there was no way I could hide it—nor did I want to—as I moved in front of Max and backed him up against the bed's footboard.

His breath caught as his back hit the wood. "You're, um... You're—"

"Naked?"

Max chewed on his lower lip as he nodded. He wasn't the kind of guy that was easily distracted or pushed around, but one of the things I was enjoying the most about him was how damn pliant he became when he was aroused or turned on.

"You snuck downstairs in the middle of the night and into my bedroom—you knew exactly what you'd find."

He opened his mouth as if to respond, but when I wedged a foot between his, he sucked in a breath and said on a rush of air, "Oh sweet Jesus..."

I chuckled. "*That's* who you expected to find?"

Max's hands moved to my hips, and as his warm fingers met my skin, it was my turn to groan. I hadn't been lying when I told him I got lonely out here, but it went beyond the companionship. Sometimes it was just nice to be touched.

"No," he said, his fingers tracing circles over my skin. "I knew exactly who I'd find in here. I just didn't expect you to be naked. You seemed so shocked yesterday when I slept that way."

"Well, we weren't friends then."

"Friends?" Max scoffed. "Is that what we are now?"

"Aren't we?"

Max lowered his eyes. "Very *naked* friends."

"Want me to go and put some clothes on?"

"Not even if the house was on fire."

I raised a brow. "Wait, you didn't ignite anything out there, did you?"

Max's fingers trailed around my hip, and when they reached the short curls surrounding the base of my dick, my hips jerked forward.

"Nope." His voice was a little raspier now as he licked his lips. "Only in here. But just so we're clear, what we're about to do right now has nothing to do with—"

"Business?" I nodded and leaned in to press my lips by his temple. "For the first time ever, I agree with you. This is going to be all about pleasure."

I let go of the bedframe to reach for his face, and Max's eyes fluttered shut. I crushed my mouth on top of his, and Max wrapped his fingers around my length.

His touch felt amazing, warm and firm, as he squeezed and worked my arousal. I shoved my tongue between his lips and reveled in the taste of him—mulled cider.

This was the last place I'd ever expected to end up with Maxwell Scott. Between the unexpected nature of his arrival and the arguments surrounding his reason for being here, my wanting to rip his clothes off right now shouldn't have happened. But as he let go of me to grab my ass and pull me closer, I decided to give in to the moment and stop trying to make sense of it all.

I rubbed my erection against his lounge pants and felt the steely length of his own desire throbbing against me. The friction of the soft material felt unbelievable, and the desire to just pin him in place and get myself off was overwhelmingly strong.

The sexy grunts and moans coming from him, however, made me want to see what Max looked like when he finally let go and stopped using that business-minded brain of his. So I slipped my hands beneath his pants and grabbed a handful of his backside, tugging him tight so I could grind up hard against him.

"Oh God," he said, and tore his mouth away. His head fell back, and I began to kiss my way along his jaw. "I should've known you'd be huge *every*where..."

I chuckled and continued kissing my way down his neck. "That going to be a problem?"

"Only if you stop."

I nipped at his chin and then looked him in the eye. "Not a snowball's chance of that happening."

A flash of fire flickered in Max's eyes. "Thank Christmas miracles for that."

"Thought you didn't believe in those."

"I don't, but it seems like the kind of thing you'd want me to say."

I chuckled and took a couple of steps back. Just as Max was about to protest, I flicked on the floor lamp in the corner of the room. A soft glow lit the space, and as my eyes drank in the gorgeous man at the foot of my bed, I reached for my eager hard-on.

It'd been a long time since I'd been intimate with anyone, and I wasn't the kind of person to go looking for a one-night stand. But from the second Max set foot on my property, the sparks had been instantaneous.

Sure, there had been back-and-forth shots taken at one another, but even then I'd felt an instant chemistry with this man, one that I was about to give in to now.

"Wow." Max lowered his eyes down to my eager cock. "Your body is... *Wow*."

"Thanks. I wish I could say the same, but..."

Max frowned, but when I gestured to his clothing he

seemed to realize he was still fully dressed. "You asking me to take off my clothes, Mr. Noble?"

"Well, you are the one who pointed out we are very *naked* friends, but so far only one of us is naked."

"Good point." He reached for the hem of his tank and drew it up over his head, and those sexy, tight muscles of his came into view.

My pulse raced. His smooth, hairless body was the complete opposite to mine, which had a dusting of dark hair covering it, and the idea of him writhing all over me made me swallow back a growl.

"Should I keep going?"

I knew I'd been caught staring. But I wasn't about to apologize. No siree.

"If you don't, I'm going to throw you out in the snow."

"Oh, threats now, huh? Well, since I don't want to lose anything important to frostbite..." Max slipped his thumbs into his waistband and pushed his pants down his legs.

He stepped out of them, and his cock sprang free. Long and hard, it jutted out from his magnificent body and all but pointed me out as the culprit to its eagerness. I was more than willing to beg for its forgiveness.

I held my hand out to Max and led him up the side of the bed. We stopped by the pulled-back covers, where I took his face between my hands and brushed a kiss across his lips. "Still don't believe in Christmas miracles?"

"I'm getting there."

"Well then, let's see if I can get you *all* the way there."

MAXWELL

GOOD GOD THIS *man is sexy as hell,* I thought as Micah lifted the sheets and I slid in beside him. I'd never seen such a perfectly sculpted body in all my life. I'd known from the way he filled out that lumberjack ensemble that he was in incredible shape, but seeing him naked? It was hard to believe he was real.

And speaking of hard...

His erection rubbed against my thigh as he pulled me in close, letting the covers drop down over us before taking my mouth in a kiss that made me almost forget where I was.

If I'd been nervous about coming down here and waking him up, I really shouldn't have been, because Micah's lips were warm and ready, moving against mine like he'd been up for hours, the same as me, just thinking of doing what we were doing right then.

As his tongue dipped into my mouth, I moaned,

reaching for his hips to pull him tighter against me. But my hands being so close to his ass was a temptation I couldn't resist, and I slid my fingers lower, to his round, smooth cheeks. I squeezed, and his cock jerked against me. Before I knew what was happening, he'd ripped his mouth away and pulled me on top of him.

"Really," I said with a grin as I straddled his hips. "And here I thought you were a top."

"Oh yeah? Then I suppose it's a good thing I am." Then he wrapped his large hand around my dick, giving it a tug that made my head fall back.

I cursed. "Do it again."

"Only if you look at me."

As soon as I met Micah's gaze, the fire in his eyes told me to get ready, because this was going to be one of the hottest nights of my life.

Bring...it...on.

I rolled my hips over Micah's, my cock still firmly in his grasp while his rubbed along the crack of my ass, and the friction was driving me out of my mind. Since the moment I saw him, I'd wondered what it would be like to be the man in his bed, and thinking about it after our kiss earlier had forced my feet to move downstairs. Something I wasn't regretting at all.

"Mmm." Micah arched up into me as he bit down on his lower lip. "You are a sexy Scrooge, aren't you?"

"Isn't Scrooge pretty selfish? I think I'm being pretty damn generous right now."

"That you are," he said, sitting up so he could take my mouth with his again.

It was so easy to fall into his kiss; it was passionate and

intense, but something about it felt so familiar, almost like home.

I heard Micah opening a drawer beside the bed and rummage through it, but I didn't care what he was doing while I was tangling my tongue with his. He could be grabbing a rope to use on me later for all I cared; nothing was going to distract me from taking what I wanted from the temptation between my thighs. Already the evidence of my arousal was making a sticky mess against his abs, but hell, they were hard enough that I could use them to get off if I wasn't so dead set on feeling his cock inside me.

A shiver racked my body as Micah released his hold on me. When I saw the lube and condom on the bed, I grabbed them up before he could and shifted down his thighs.

He raised a brow at my eagerness, and I gave him a mischievous grin before pushing him back down on the bed.

"You've wanted to put me to work the whole time I've been here. You wouldn't deprive me of getting my hands dirty for once, would you?"

Micah grinned and moved his arms behind his head. "Maxwell Scott getting dirty? What did I do to deserve such a thing?"

"Did you just call me Maxwell?"

"Is that really what you wanna talk about right now?" His gaze dropped to the condom wrapper in my hand and the insistent kick of his erection demanding attention.

Hell, he could call me whatever he wanted with a dick like that.

I tore open the packet and went to slide it on, but the

glistening, plump tip had my mouth watering. Leaning down over him, I swiped my tongue over the head, getting a good taste before sliding the condom down his large length.

Jesus, I didn't even know if I could handle all those inches, but since there was nothing I loved more than a challenge, I quickly lubed him up before reaching around to do the same to myself.

"Damn that's hot." Micah was looking at me with eyes full of arousal. If I could've taken a mental snapshot right then I would've, because that look was one I'd definitely want to carry for future use.

"You ready for me?" As I rose to my knees, hovering over his hips, I swirled my finger around the head of his dick, teasing him even though it was torture for me to wait any longer to have him inside me.

Micah growled and then grabbed my hips, ready to take control, but I was feeling as greedy as he was and lowered myself slowly onto him.

Wow. The sheer size of him filled me completely, and I had to remind myself to breathe as I took him in inch by inch. The burn wasn't at all unpleasant, though, not when I was as hot and ready for Micah as I was.

"So good," Micah managed, the cords of his neck strained as he gripped my hips hard. "Take it all."

I could feel the sweat beading on my brow, but I ignored it, too focused on relishing how amazing it felt to be consumed by the gorgeous man beneath me. The gorgeous, *bossy* man.

But this was one time I was fine with taking orders, and

I bore down and took in every inch of him. My eyes fluttered closed as I breathed, enjoying the way he felt inside me. The hunger was growing, though, the need to come now dominating my thoughts.

I began to rock a little before rolling my hips, adjusting and accommodating Micah's length before rising until only the tip remained inside me.

He moaned from the loss, but when I drove back down on him again, he sucked in a breath and closed his eyes.

"I don't think so," I said, panting. "Keep those eyes on me."

Heat flared in his gaze, and as I began to ride him, he kept one hand on my hips and brought the other down to take hold of my cock. The pre-cum was making a mess of him already, but it also made for an easier slide, and on every thrust I pumped my dick through his tight fist.

Dammit. The sensation of feeling Micah everywhere was almost too much.

That look he gave me as he watched me, though... That look was going to send me over the edge.

I licked my lips as the intensity built, not wanting this to be over so soon, but knowing there was no way I could delay it for much longer. Apparently my body had wanted Micah for longer than my brain had realized, and now that this was happening, I couldn't stop the orgasm from threatening.

"Shit...Micah—"

"I'm right there with you, Max," he said, breathing hard. "It's too good... Fuck."

I clenched my ass around him, and that was all it took.

A roar left him as he came, and the pulsing from his dick had me joining him only seconds later.

As the orgasm hit, my cum exploded out onto his hand and chest, yet I continued to ride him, taking every last bit of his arousal from him until we both couldn't move anymore.

I collapsed in exhaustion on top of him, for once not caring at all about the mess. How could I when I could barely lift my head?

"That was..." I tried to think of what to say, but nothing came. "I think I've lost my words. You've fucked the words out of me."

"Looks like my evil plan worked all along." Micah chuckled, but it was an exhausted sound that made me grin.

"Hold on. Did I wear out the lumberjack? Is that even possible?"

"Can you blame me with all that foreplay? You've been teasing my dick since you arrived."

"It wasn't intentional. Just my magnetic charm." It was too bad he couldn't see my smirk as I turned my head to the side on his chest, only to frown.

Snoopy laid at the foot of the bed, eyes closed and sleeping soundly despite the frenzy we'd just caused.

"Uh, has Snoopy been there the whole time?"

Micah glanced down and laughed. "Looks like it."

"You sure he's not dead?"

"Nah."

"Damn." I was finally able to lift my head enough to look at Micah, and he had that look on his face again. "Not that I'm trying to kill myself, so give me ten, but you think he'll mind us having a round two?" I asked.

"Not in the fucking least." Micah hauled me up his body and pulled me in for another kiss, one I knew would lead to nothing but more trouble, but at that moment, it was exactly the kind of trouble I couldn't get enough of.

"MERRY CHRISTMAS, SLEEPYHEAD," I said the next morning as Max shuffled out of my room, hair wild and pajamas back on. I'd fully expected to sleep hard after our, well, busy night, but I'd only managed maybe a couple hours before giving up on any shuteye.

Max, however, had passed out the moment his head hit the pillow. As I watched him, my thoughts had run away from me. First I relished every second of the night, from the dance to the kiss to his sneaking into my bed. But then I'd think about the fact that he'd be leaving, and that the last thing I needed to do was get attached to someone I wouldn't see again.

Or, in Max's case, someone who still worked for a company that wanted to buy me out. Was that still what he wanted? Or had his time here convinced him that the town was best left as it was?

I felt a niggle of guilt about being the reason why he

was still here, and on Christmas at that, but I pushed that aside as I stood up and poured us both mugs of coffee. After all, he hadn't seemed too upset about missing holidays with his family, if that was something he even did. He'd shut me down when I asked about it before, but maybe now he'd be more forthcoming about his personal life.

"Look at you," Max said. "Up before dawn even on Christmas."

"Before dawn? It's the late hour of"—I checked the clock—"nine thirty."

"Wow, letting me sleep in? It *must* be Christmas."

"I just figured you might be exhausted from your late-night workout."

A flush hit Max's cheeks, and it was so unexpected— and cute as hell—that I moved toward him. He looked up at me as I cupped his cheek, and as our mouths met, I fell into the softness of his lips.

"Mmm. Now that's a good way to wake up," Max said. "And last night wasn't a bad way to fall asleep, either."

I chuckled and headed to the fridge. "Well, I'm glad it 'wasn't bad' for you. That's high praise in your book, right?"

"Huuuge praise." He gave me a wink before taking a long sip of his coffee.

I stirred some snow cream into my mug, tasted it, then added a little more. "I'd caffeine up if I were you."

He looked at me over his mug. "Oh? Is there a round three I should know about?"

"Actually, there is." But before he could get excited about that, I added, "With my siblings."

"No offense, your family's great, but I'm not really up for a group situation. Freak."

I chuckled and shook my head. "You've met them a couple of times now, but we always get together Christmas Day, and if you're up for it, I'd love for you to join us. It's super casual, pajamas preferred, and no working whatsoever. Promise."

"So you want me to go over to your family's house...in this." Max gestured to his lounge pants and tank top.

I stroked my beard. "Okay, we might need to cover the top half of you up a little more if I want to stay decent around the family, but nothing fancy or formal."

Max smirked, and it was all I could do not to grab him and kiss it right off his lips. "So how much time do I have?"

"About thirty minutes less than you would if we'd arrived on time."

"What?" Max's eyes widened. "We were supposed to be there thirty minutes ago?"

I shrugged, not concerned in the least that I was missing out on the argument as to who would shovel the walkway.

Max put his mug on the counter and aimed an accusatory look my way. "Why didn't you tell me?"

"And when was I supposed to do that? Last night when you were sneaking in my room? Or when you stripped and straddled my—"

"How about this morning when *you* woke up?"

"You were sleeping."

"Uuugh." Max bristled, and I couldn't help but think how cute he looked frustrated. Funny how much could change in a couple of days. "You didn't think that maybe you should wake me up so I had time to get ready?"

"No. And why are you so worried, anyway?"

"*Um*, maybe because your siblings already hate me. And now they're *really* going to hate me."

He wasn't wrong about that. My family had a tendency to become a little protective when someone was trying to buy their family home and turn it into a resort. But one thing I knew he wasn't thinking about was my sudden desire to protect *him*. "I won't let anything happen to you, I promise."

"Happen to me?" The alarm in Max's voice made me laugh. "Like what?"

"Don't you need to go and get ready?"

"Oh, yeah, you're right." He turned to head over to the stairs, and at the last second stopped and looked back at me. "Are you trying to avoid the question?"

Smart man... "No."

"You're lying." Max shook his head. "You're totally lying. They're going to play some horrible prank on me, aren't they?"

"Like?"

"Oh, I don't know." He threw his hands in the air and began stomping up the stairs. "But don't think I wouldn't have suspected them about my car if they'd been around. Especially your sister Gina!"

I cringed as Max disappeared from view, and went back to finishing my coffee. That was the second time in a matter of days he'd mentioned that blasted car of his, and the niggling guilt in my stomach was starting to feel real uncomfortable.

I rinsed our mugs out and put them in the sink to dry, and as I crossed the living room, about to grab my boots, I heard from the top of the stairs: "Micah?"

I stopped to peer up to the second floor, expecting to see Max at the top, but the landing was empty.

"This fiddly shower of yours is acting up! I think I need you to come up here and fix it for me."

I shouldn't... I thought, that guilt from a second ago intensifying at the idea of Max finding out he was stuck here because of me. But then I heard the water turn on and thought, what the hell—I was already going on the naughty list this year; might as well make it count.

O KAY, SO MAYBE joining Max in the shower hadn't been the smartest decision in terms of being on time, but it had been worth it.

As Max and I headed up Gina's driveway, I tried not to laugh from the way he slid all over the place. I would've helped steady him if my arms weren't already full of bags of presents, which at the moment were in danger of dropping all over the place due to the death grip he had on my arm.

"I want a broken tailbone for Christmaaas," Max sang, totally off-key, but hey, at least he had the gist of the Hippopotamus song right. And here I thought he didn't know any Christmas songs.

The front door opened wide as soon as we stepped onto the porch. Gina had her hands on her hips and wore a sweatshirt saying, "Mama needs a silent night."

"Well, well, well. Look who finally decided to show up. Did you get lost? You only live down the street, you know."

"Nice shirt," I said, ignoring her scowl as I gave her a kiss on the cheek.

"That's not an 'I'm sorry,' Micah."

"Merry Christmas, Gina. You remember I have company, right?" I gestured for Max to join me, and Gina's brows rose.

Luckily she didn't say anything snarky about the fact that Max was not only still in town, but also joining me for the holiday gathering. Instead she gave me a look that said we'd talk later and then managed a smile and greeting for Max.

"Yep. She's definitely pranking me today," Max whispered as I set the bags down to take off my jacket.

"If that happens, you'll just have to get her back. I'll even help you."

Interest flared in his eyes. "Reallyyy..."

"Uncle Micaaah!" Three little rugrats dove at my legs, wrapping their arms around my calves as they held on tight. "Come see what Santa brought."

I pretended to struggle to lift my leg. "I think you munchkins have grown a foot overnight. Can't...move..."

Giggles rang out as they tightened their grips, and as I began to walk down the hall much like Frankenstein's monster, Max grabbed the bags of presents and followed us into the living room.

Torn wrapping paper was everywhere, covering every inch of the floor, along with all the new toys they'd gotten. Gina's husband Bob sat on the couch, in deep conversation with Travis, both of them holding on to empty trash bags like the women of the family had sent them in there to clean up but they hadn't quite gotten that far yet.

Travis looked up as we all lumbered in, and the kids let go of me to race for the first things they wanted to show off.

"Hey, you missed the morning massacre," he said, getting up to give me a hug.

I gestured to the mess. "Doesn't look like I missed anything."

"We saved it all for you," Bob said, slapping the garbage bag to my chest and grinning. "Merry Christmas."

I glanced over my shoulder to Max, who was wide-eyed and taking it all in. "I'm loved. Can you tell?"

Before he could answer, I was surrounded by the chaos kiddos, each shoving themselves in front of the other to show off their toys.

"Hey, hey, one at a time," I said, and then waved Max over. "And I want you to meet my friend Max. He'd love to see what Santa brought you, too."

Out of the corner of my eye I saw Travis and Bob exchanging a look, but kids didn't discriminate, and soon Max and I found ourselves on the wrapping-paper-covered floor entertaining my nieces and nephews while the gossip crew, otherwise known as my sisters, watched from the kitchen.

Oh, I was gonna hear about it soon, but for now I was content to watch the city boy beside me play with my nephew's train set and—hopefully—rediscover what a real family Christmas was all about.

MAXWELL

"EVERYONE OUT!"

I winced at the volume of Gina's voice as I stepped inside the kitchen, and watched as she held a pot up over her head and moved toward the sink.

"I swear, if I trip over any of you, I will take away all the presents Santa brought and replace them with lumps of coal."

I believed her, too. Out of all of Micah's siblings, Gina scared me the most.

As the kids raced out of the small space, she emptied the cooked potatoes into the waiting colander.

What on earth had I done to Micah to deserve the task of assisting his sister in the kitchen? I shrank back against the door, hoping to go undetected, but as if she had eyes in the back of her head, Gina said, "You going to just stand there? Or do you plan to make yourself useful?"

Well, shit. I pushed off the door and told myself to stop acting like a coward.

You deal with money-hungry sharks every day of the week. You can handle Gina.

As I stepped up beside her, she held out the potato masher, but before I could take it she narrowed her eyes on me and gave me a slow once-over full of judgment. "What do you think you're doing?"

I looked around the kitchen and then back to the cooking utensil. "Uh, I figured you wanted me to maybe mash the potatoes."

She handed me the masher. "Don't get smart with me, Mr. Corporate."

"Um..." I swallowed and gestured to the masher. "I'm not. I just... I'm a little confused. What do you mean, what am I doing?"

Gina shook her head, and let out a sigh. "With *Micah?*"

Huh?

"Anyone with half a brain can see that the two of you are a lot 'friendlier' than the last time we saw you, so again I ask, what do you think you're doing?"

Shit. Shit. Oh shit... I looked over to the door, hoping and praying for one of those Christmas miracles Micah was so fond of, but I was out of luck. No one burst through to interrupt this awkward moment, and no one was here to get me out of it.

I had no idea how to respond to this. What was I doing with Micah? As of last night, anything and everything he'd let me. The man was a walking billboard for hot, sexy lumberjacks, and for some reason he'd decided to let me climb all over him. But somehow I didn't think that would go over all that well with his sister.

"I'm not doing anything." *...that he doesn't want me to.* "We just decided to call a kind of truce while I'm here."

Yes, that was what I'd call hot sex in his bed, the shower, and hopefully later tonight by the fireplace...a truce.

"I hardly think Micah is the type to call a truce with someone who wants to buy his house and bulldoze it to the *ground*."

I jerked back as though she'd slapped me. Something about those words stung this time around. Even though they were right on point. I *did* want to bulldoze his house to the ground. Well, not me personally, but still.

"Try again," she said, crossing her arms and tapping her foot against the kitchen floor.

I opened my mouth, about to do just that, when the kitchen door swung open and—thank you, baby Jesus— Micah and Taylor walked in laughing with one another. When Micah caught sight of me with a masher in one hand and Gina giving me the stink eye, he stopped in his tracks.

"Uh, everything okay in here?" he said.

I swallowed hard as I looked at Gina and then at the potatoes straining in the sink. "I was just asking Gina where I can find the"—*what the hell goes in potatoes?*— "butter?"

Micah looked over my shoulder at the potatoes and suppressed a grin. "Maybe mash those first and then you can get your hands dirty."

Shit, there he went again, making double entendres and sending my mind back to a place it didn't need to be with his protective sister on attack.

"Actually," Gina said, "I was just asking Max why the two of you seem so cozy all of a sudden when the whole reason he's here is to get you to sign papers."

Well, that was one thing about Micah's sister I could respect: you never had to guess how she really felt.

"Gina, not now—" Micah started, but she waved him off as Lana walked into the kitchen.

"No, we should get all this out in the open," Taylor said before pinning me with a stern look. "We know you're here to try to take everything our brother loves most in the world, and just so you know, it's not happening. Not on our watch."

Gina nodded. "Don't think your pretty face is going to do you any favors. Micah may be the sweetest of the bunch, but you still have to get through us to get to him."

"Aren't we gonna talk about the elephant in the room?" Lana said, a sly smile on her face, one that made the blood rush to mine.

Did she know about last night? How?

She flipped her hair over her shoulder, her smile growing. "You two are busted. I saw you dancing last night."

Micah rolled his eyes. "So? It was a dance. That's what you're supposed to do."

"Nooo, not the dancing. The *kissing*."

Gina's jaw dropped to the floor, but Taylor nodded like she already knew.

When no one said anything, I felt like I needed to help in some way. "There was mistletoe."

All eyes shot in my direction, and I never realized how intimidating a pack of women could be.

"You *kissed* him?" Gina swatted Micah on the arm as the other two joined in asking questions a mile a minute.

"All right, all right, everyone zip it for five seconds," Micah said over them, and to my surprise, their mouths snapped shut. He glanced at me. "Fine. Yes. Since you three can't seem to be like Travis and stay out of my business, there was a kiss. Yes, there's an attraction. No, I'm not under any delusions Max didn't come here with a purpose."

"You don't think that means seducing you to get what he wants?" Gina said.

Micah's gaze fell on me once more, like the thought hadn't even occurred to him, and it definitely hadn't occurred to me, either.

"I'd never do that," I said. "I may be a lot of things, but that's too devious for me. And no matter what I think of your brother, I'll keep business separate from any personal...dealings."

"*Dealings?*" Taylor snorted and looked at Micah. "He just equated your kiss to a business deal."

I winced, not having meant it that way at all, but then Micah decided to throw in his two cents.

"If that's the case, I'm going to say he certainly knows how to...close a deal."

My cheeks flushed as all the girls' jaws hit the floor, but when Micah winked at me, I almost melted to the ground in a heap. Damn, what was this guy doing to me?

Micah held his hand out, and when I took it he reached for the masher and shoved it toward Taylor.

"Here, I'm going to save Max and leave you ladies to process all of this. Good? Good."

When they all just continued to stare, I waved and followed Micah out of the kitchen. I was about to ask him what in the world he was thinking, all but spelling out what we did last night, when he pulled open a small door and yanked me inside.

I tumbled inside the... I had no idea where I was.

Micah reached around me and flicked on a light. It was storage under the stairs.

"Are you crazy?" I said. "Your sisters already think I'm trying to seduce you, and now you're pulling me into closets."

Micah, the smug bastard, flashed a handsome grin and then placed a hand on either side of the door by my head. "You're telling me you're *not* trying to seduce me out of my property? Now that is a shame."

"You know I'm not. We promised last night—"

"And this morning."

"—*and* this morning were about pleasure. Not business."

"So we did, which is why I pulled you in here. I want to make sure you're okay. That my sisters didn't hurt your feelings or scare you off."

My lips twitched. "*That's* why you pulled me in here?"

"Well, part of it. The other part is this." Micah lowered his head and brushed his lips over mine, and my heart began to thump.

I reached for his sweater and curled my fingers into the warm wool. This was the kind of kiss you dreamed about. The kind that you saw in movies. My toes curled in my shoes, then Micah raised his head and bumped his nose to mine.

"I just wanted you to know that I never, for one second, thought you were sleeping with me for a business deal."

I bit down on my lip. Those words meant so much more to me than I had expected. "I know that."

"Do you?"

"Yes. Of course."

"Okay." Micah took a step back, tracing his fingers down my cheek, and my stomach flipped. Something about the way he was looking at me had me feeling...nervous? No, that wasn't the right word. He was making me feel vulnerable.

"Um, don't you think we should maybe join them before they get the wrong idea?"

"Probably." Micah reached around me and took hold of the handle, then said against my lips, "But if being with you is wrong, then I don't know what's so good about being right."

LUCKILY, WE HADN'T gotten busted in the closet, and an hour later we were seated around a long table in the dining room. The kids had scampered off to their own little table, where I had no doubt there'd be a mess for their parents to clean up after. When I first walked into the dining room, I'd almost considered joining them, at least if the inquisitors—also known as Micah's sisters—were still up to playing one hundred questions.

But other than a few looks in our direction when they thought we weren't paying attention, they hadn't said so much as a peep, not about anything to do with my and Micah's current situation.

When they weren't being overprotective and threatening, it was actually nice to see how the entire family interacted. To hear their jokes, many of which, I had a feeling, had longtime hidden meanings. To watch the way they'd scoop an extra helping of potatoes onto another's plate because they knew it was their favorite.

I'd never experienced anything like it. I didn't have brothers or sisters to talk to or lean on or laugh with. My idea of a family dinner was sitting at the end of a long table with a nanny while my parents worked late, or whatever it was they did. I wouldn't know, because we rarely spoke about anything of consequence.

I bit down on my lip as I stabbed at a few green beans. *Don't get emotional, for fuck's sake. It's not like you've had a bad life.*

But the fact that it was Christmas and my parents probably didn't even notice? It just showed how different Micah and I had grown up and the extremes in how we lived our respective lives. His world revolved around his loved ones and his family home. Mine revolved around... myself. Getting a partnership, making money, those were my goals. They couldn't be further from Micah's.

I glanced at him giving his full attention to whatever his brother-in-law was saying. But the moment he felt my stare, Micah looked my way, and I knew I was in trouble.

"Everything okay?" he whispered, giving my thigh a reassuring squeeze.

"Yeah...of course." There was no way I was going to admit that this whole scene had me nostalgic for something I'd never had. I cleared my throat and pointed at my plate with my fork to change the subject. "This is really great."

"Yeah? What would you be eating if you weren't here? Wait, no, let me guess. A piece of really expensive steak... maybe with, like, something fancy like truffle butter sauce, am I right?"

I forced a smile. "Nailed it."

And he had. The only thing he hadn't added was my eating it out of a to-go box alone in my apartment.

"Okay, family, it's that time," Gina said, grabbing her glass of wine. "We forgot to do it at Thanksgiving because we're heathens, so let's go around and say what we're grateful for this year. I'll start: I'm grateful that even though I have three of the wildest children known to man, that every day when I pick them up from school, they aren't embarrassed at all to give their mom a big hug and kiss." She flicked away a tear and sniffed. "It won't last, so dammit, I'm going to enjoy it. Next."

As each person went down the line, I felt a sense of panic. What in the world could I possibly say that wouldn't make me sound like a giant douchebag?

I was grateful for all the deals I'd made this year. The gorgeous penthouse apartment I had moved into. The new office my company had decided to upgrade to—and, oh yeah, the really hot sex I'd had last night. But none of that was very appropriate for a Christmas meal declaration. Shit.

As I sat there listening to how Micah was grateful that they'd raised enough money from the Christmas tree farm to be able to donate to the local school for their new arts facility, my douchebag-meter was right off the scale—then it was my turn.

"Max?" Gina said, her tone speaking volumes as she looked my way. She *knew* I was struggling to think of something.

"Um, what I'm grateful for..." I looked around the table at all the eyes aimed in my direction—and when my gaze fell on Micah, bingo, I had it. "I'm grateful that my car decided to break down *after* I reached Micah's place. Otherwise I would've been stranded in the middle of nowhere in a snowstorm with no cell service *and* I wouldn't be spending this lovely Christmas with all of you."

Silence fell around the table as everyone's attention shifted to Micah. *What the hell?* I frowned, thinking back over what I'd just said, then turned to see Micah glaring back at all his siblings. What was going on?

Micah quickly cleared his throat and plastered on a smile. "I'm, um, I'm grateful for that too."

"Yeah," I scoffed. "I can totally tell."

Micah started to laugh and reached under the table to squeeze my leg. "No, I really do mean it. I'm glad you're here with us and had a chance to experience the tree farm at Christmas, truly I am."

I smiled and nodded, relief filling me. I hadn't made a fool out of myself. I went back to finishing off my meal.

It was surprising how an act of fate had led me here to this little town, and to this very table, and while my reasons for first coming out here were still there, I found they weren't quite as important to me as what I'd gained over the last few days—a little bit of Christmas magic.

MAX HAD BEEN quiet on the drive home. When we got here he'd helped me bring in a few logs before disappearing upstairs, and I wondered if I or one of my siblings had done something to upset him. He'd seemed fine the rest of the day, even getting down on the floor to play with the kids for a bit, but I could tell he'd gone inward somehow, and I didn't know what had set him off.

I was stoking the fire when I heard the sound of footsteps on the old stairs. A few seconds later Max sat down on the floor beside me, crossing his legs and leaning back on his hands. He didn't say anything, seemingly content to just watch what I was doing.

Glancing down, I noticed he'd changed into a long-sleeved thermal shirt, making himself comfortable. What a change from the man who'd shown up practically living in a tailored suit.

"You've gone quiet tonight," I said without looking his

way. I didn't want to come off as accusatory, only curious what was on his mind. He was definitely in his head about something, but I couldn't pinpoint what that was exactly.

"Am I? Sorry."

"You don't have to apologize. Just an observation." I gave the fire one last jab and set the poker back in its holder. "Anything you want to talk about? My family drive you crazy?"

Max cracked a smile. "No, your family's great."

"Really. So their interrogation didn't upset you?"

"Not at all. I kinda like that they were ready to kick my ass to protect you. You're lucky. It made me wish I had someone in my corner who'd be willing to do the same."

"You don't?"

"I'm an only child."

"What about your parents? Are you guys close?"

Max rubbed at his face. "Well, it's Christmas, and even if my phone had service it wouldn't have gone off today anyway. So, no, we're not close."

"Did something happen or... I mean, has it always been that way?"

"It's just how things are." Max focused on picking the lint off his pants, trying to seem unbothered, but I could hear the hurt in his voice. "I didn't realize other people grew up different, that a family could come together on a holiday just to eat and spend time together. You've said you do that some days for no reason at all. I never understood what that was like until today, I guess. So, yeah. You're lucky."

My impulse to make some kind of joke about being stuck with three gossipy sisters and a shit-stirring brother was right there on the tip of my tongue, but something about Max's tone told me now wasn't the time.

This was more a confession of sorts, one of the first honest-to-God insights as to who this man was, and I wasn't about to brush it off with some lame joke just because it would be easier.

"You're right. I am lucky in the sense I have family close by and ones that I love spending time with. Holidays are fun, and watching the kiddos grow up is something I wouldn't change for the world. But it hasn't always felt that way. The year we lost our parents was particularly hard."

Max looked at me.

"You can ask," I said.

He opened his mouth and then quickly shut it, frowning. "I don't want to bring up something painful for you. Not on Christmas."

I reached for his hand and laced my fingers through his. "It's not painful to talk about them. Not anymore. And we're talking about family. They were, and still are, a big part of that."

Max nodded as I stroked my thumb over the back of his hand.

"This cabin, the property? It belonged to them, and my grandparents before that. I told you, several of us were born—"

"Yeah, in the barn. I remember."

I grinned and nodded. "One of the horse stalls, actually, so don't panic about where you were dancing last night."

"Good to know."

"Yeah. They loved this place. It was in their blood, and as a result, it ended up being in all of ours. The trees, the magic, the sense of community this place instilled in us. That was all them. Then one night, on the way home from town, their car swerved off the road, and just like that, we lost them." I paused for a second and looked to the crackling fire. "It was unreal, unfathomable that they weren't here with us anymore, but this farm, and this...place? This is all them, they're here with us everywhere you look, and that's why—"

"You'll never sell this place..."

I nodded. "Right."

He let out a breath and scooted in closer to me, wrapping his arm around mine. "See, that's what I mean. These stories, these memories you have—you're lucky to have them. I don't have anything like that. Not even close."

"Surely you have some memory of your childhood that makes you smile."

Max thought for a second and then shook his head. "Nope. While your parents were raising you to understand the importance of family and community, mine were teaching me the number one rule of business. The only thing that matters is money. Because money makes you happy, haven't you heard?"

"Has it made you happy?"

Max let out a sigh and rested his head against my arm. "I *thought* it had."

"Thought? As in past tense?"

"In all honesty, I don't really think I understood what true happiness looked like until I came up here."

"Oh yeah?"

"Yeah. I thought money bought you freedom. The ability to do what you want, wear what you want, *be* who you want, and what could make a person happier than that?"

I shrugged, wondering where he was going with this. "I don't know."

"How about knowing who you are without any of that? Because I gotta say, these last few days have made me question who the hell I am. That's for sure."

As I took all that in, I felt that damn sense of guilt in the pit of my stomach again. Hadn't this been what I wanted? For Max to see how incredible this place was, what it meant to the town as well as to me? I'd never expected for that to actually happen, though. I hadn't known about his childhood or his life in Manhattan, or that a few days could really change a person's point of view. I hadn't known bringing him around my family would make him think of everything he was missing. All of this had started because I wanted to protect this place, but now that was the last thing on my mind.

I leaned my head down to rest on top of Max's where it lay on my shoulder.

"I'm glad I'm here," Max said softly, rubbing his fingers over my jean-clad thigh. "Thank you for letting me be a part of today."

"Thank you for wanting to be a part of today. No regrets?"

"Well... I could've been less of an ass when I arrived. But it did get me some fabulous new clothes."

"Oh, the clothes are fabulous now? Wow, who are you and where did Max go?" I lifted my head to grin down at him, and he looked at me in a way I couldn't read.

"I like that," he said. "That you call me Max. No one's ever called me that before."

"I thought you hated it."

"Maxwell just fits my pretentious shit image better, don't you think?"

I had to laugh, because he was right. There was no way I could've called him Maxwell with a straight face. Maxwell was the guy who came down here giving no fucks about this place, but Max? He was the guy falling in love with it.

But all that only made my guilt stronger, and with Max making a confession, it was only right that I make one of my own. It might change everything, but hopefully he wouldn't hate me when I told him.

"There's something I need to admit," I said, turning so I could look him in the eyes. "I'm not proud of it, but all this talk about you being a pretentious shit when we met... well, I thought so too. Which is why I..."

"Yeah?"

I blew out a breath and rushed through the words. "I took the spark plugs out of your car."

Whatever he'd been expecting to hear, it wasn't that, and he choked out a laugh like he thought I was joking. "You what?"

"I took the spark plugs out of your car. There wasn't anything wrong with it that I didn't have a hand in. I'm the reason you got stranded here."

Max's mouth fell open as he stared at me, and then he began to laugh. Low at first, and then a full-out belly laugh that had him falling back on the floor holding his stomach. "Oh my God," he said between fits. "You're a terrible person. Thank fuck."

"What's so funny?"

Max wiped at his eyes as he sat up and struggled to catch his breath. "This whole time I thought you were this perfect guy who donates to charity and can do no wrong, but you took the spark plugs...out of my car..." He began to wheeze again, which in turn made me laugh.

"So you're...not mad? Am I getting this right?"

"Oh, I would've been furious if I'd known before. But now it's too funny." He shook his head. "So what was it? My pain-in-the ass charm? My hot ass? My sexy smile? You couldn't seem to let me go before you got a piece of me?"

I rolled my eyes. "Yes, your ego was so appealing. I was trying to prove a point."

"And what was that point, exactly?"

"That if you spent enough time here you might realize there's more to a place than a piece of property or an opportunity."

Max chuckled and shook his head. "And you thought you'd achieve that by stealing my spark plugs."

"Well, no, I thought I'd have *time* to achieve that by stealing your spark plugs. My plan was to let the town charm you."

Max's lips twitched as he scooted back in close to me, bumping his shoulder with mine. "It wasn't only the town, you know."

I frowned down at him.

"That *charmed* me. Yes, your farm, and the dance and the mistletoe—I mean, what person in their right mind could resist that? But add in you..."

"What about me?"

Max reached out to trail his fingers down my cheek and over my beard. "You are difficult to...ignore."

"If this is a joke about my size—"

"It should be. But it's not. It's about you as a person, Micah. From the second I showed up here, you've been nothing but gracious, even when you wanted to toss me out on my ass. You gave me a place to sleep, the clothes out of your damn closet, and no matter how much I tried to fight you, that charm of yours won me over."

Max leaned in and ghosted his lips over mine.

"You said you'd sweep me off my feet, and you were right. Christmas was nothing but an inconvenience to me before, but you made me realize that's not true. Christmas is about love and caring. About magic. There was none of that before, but here? Here I feel the magic. You gave that to me."

I placed my hand over his where it rested on my cheek, and as I moved to deepen the kiss, Max smiled against my mouth.

"You still have those spark plugs, right?"

I didn't bother with an answer as I took his lips in one of the sweetest kisses I'd ever had and gently lowered him to his back—and it was tempting to "accidentally" lose the spark plugs so I could keep him here a little longer.

MAXWELL

$\mathcal{I}$ WOKE THE next morning to an empty bed—
Micah's empty bed. He was such an early bird
that it wasn't much of a surprise, but I wouldn't have
minded spending a few more hours with him between the
sheets. Instead, Snoopy had taken up the warm spot he'd
left, and though he'd probably be a decent cuddler, I had to
get back home soon and didn't want to spend the last few
hours I had left with anyone but Micah.

So I forced myself out of the bed and threw some
clothes on before heading into the kitchen, thinking I'd
find him drinking coffee. But the house was quiet, with
only the crackling of a low fire in the living room.

He had to be outside, then. As much as I dreaded being
out in the snow this early in the morning, I'd be a trooper,
dammit.

I shoved into a pair of boots by the door and wrapped
myself up in the thickest coat I could find, and then I
stepped out onto the porch.

While it was still cold, the sun was shining brightly and had melted much of the snow away. I scanned the yard, not seeing any sign of Micah until my eyes landed on the carport where my Lexus had been parked since I arrived. And wouldn't you know it, there was that troublemaker, shutting the hood. He reached for a rag out of his pocket, and as he wiped his hands off on it, he looked up, and a smile slowly crossed his face.

"What'd you remove this time?" I called out as I made my way over to him, which was much easier to do without a foot or two of snow to wade through.

"The engine. You didn't need that, did you?"

"Nah, I'm sure it'll work fine without it. Not that I know much about cars or anything."

That sexy grin on his face was nearly enough to make me swoon. I wouldn't have minded if he really had taken my car apart, if it meant he wanted to keep me here.

"Everything's back in order, just the way it was when you got here," Micah said. "And look—you won't even need snow tires for the drive home."

Several days ago that would've been music to my ears. I hadn't wanted to get stuck here; I'd wanted luxury accommodations and a signature. But now just hearing Micah talk about my driving home made me feel sick to my stomach.

I'd been here long enough; I knew that. I'd be expected back at work and things would return to my old normal. But I couldn't deny how much I'd miss the man I'd come to know in only a handful of days. We were so different, our lives polar opposites, and that should be enough reason to drive away easily. Nothing about this situation would be easy, though, at least for me. I hadn't even left yet and already I felt a homesickness like I'd never known.

How was that possible?

"You kicking me out?"

Micah walked over to me, tucking the rag in his back pocket, before shoving his hands into the pockets of his jacket. "Thought you'd see it more like giving you a means to escape."

I cocked my head, looking up at him, and while there was a smile on those full lips, I could see the melancholy in his eyes. But I wasn't about to let our last couple of minutes or hours be spent focused on the bad, not when we'd come as far as we had.

I reached for his jacket and pulled him in close to me. "The last thing I want to do is escape. But I'm pretty sure you know that by now."

"Oh yeah? So you going to buy a log cabin and move out here to Merrihill?"

I chuckled. The idea of that was not as ludicrous as it was a couple of days ago. "Why? You know one that's for sale?"

Micah's eyes darkened and the sadness from seconds ago hardened.

Shit. "I didn't mean—"

"Nope." Micah reached for my hands and gently removed them from his lapels. "It's fine. I'm not stupid, Max. I knew this conversation was going to come up. But my answer's the same. I'm not interested in selling."

I opened my mouth, about to tell him that wasn't what

I'd been getting at, when he stepped around me and began walking back to the house.

"Micah! Wait up a second."

"I need to feed Snoopy," he called back, not bothering to stop.

Stubborn man...

I'd said it once, and I'd say it until the very end of time: Micah Noble was a stubborn, stubborn man.

I tromped after him, making my way up the stairs as the front door slammed shut. How weird; I'd almost forgotten this side of him over the last few days. The bull-headed, stubborn, pain-in-the-ass side of him. But as I knocked the last of the snow off my booted feet and made my way inside, I decided enough was enough.

"Listen," I said as I stormed inside and closed the door behind me—I knew how much Micah hated letting the warm air out. "What I said out there wasn't some kind of sneaky way of asking if you wanted to sell your farm to me. I was just making conversation. So there's no need to get your long johns in a twist."

Micah placed Snoopy's bowl down on the floor with a clang, then he straightened and looked over at me. "Okay."

"Okay?" I held my hands up. "What does that mean? Okay, you believe me? Okay, you think I'm a scheming, lying, no-good city boy? Or okay, you don't care as long as I leave as soon as humanly possible?"

Micah crossed his arms over that spectacular chest and shrugged. "It means exactly what I said: okay."

"Oh my God." I rubbed my hands over my face and bit back a frustrated growl. "I can't believe you're seriously picking a fight with me right now. After a good couple of days, why not end things with an argument? Gotcha."

I stormed across the room, fully intending on going upstairs to pack my shit, but at the last second I turned back around, too annoyed to let this go.

"Just so you know, you won, all right? Your little scheme to make me stay here and fall for you and this place worked just perfectly, didn't it? I get to go back to my job and let them know I failed. But you know what? I don't give a shit about that. I care that you're making the best decision for you and your family, and you were right, that's exactly as it should be. So keep believing I'm the bad guy with terrible intentions, you ass."

There. I'd said my piece.

I turned back toward the stairs, but Micah grabbed my arm and yanked me toward him. Before I knew what was happening, his mouth was on mine, kissing me with an unrelenting intensity that made my knees buckle. Luckily, he wrapped his strong arms around me, holding me close against him, but even if he hadn't, I wasn't going anywhere. I kissed him harder, letting all the frustration out until our frenzy turned into something more sensual, passionate.

He hadn't picked a fight with me because he wanted me to leave; he'd picked a fight because he didn't. I could feel that with every tangle of our tongues and every soft moan he made.

It wasn't right to feel a connection like this only to have to end things before they'd even started.

But as long as I was kissing him, we didn't have to face that reality, not yet. So we stayed there, wrapped up in each other as time passed. It could've been only seconds, minutes, even an hour, but it was still too soon when we pulled away from each other, sucking in gulps of air as Micah dropped his forehead to mine.

"Maybe I can stay for another day or two," I said when I found my voice.

Micah shook his head against mine. "No. That'll only make it worse."

I knew he was right. The more time I spent here, with him, the less I wanted to leave. If I didn't go now, I might never go, and this wasn't my life. It was just a nice reprieve from the chaos I lived in, with a beautiful man who was pure and good and true—and occasionally an ass, albeit a sexy one. That combination wasn't one I thought I'd come across again, but finding love hadn't been my focus in life.

Reluctantly I pulled away, averting my eyes. "Let me just go grab a couple things and I'll head out."

"Max, you don't have to leave right this minute—"

"I do. I need to get on the road before it decides to snow again."

Before he could try to disagree, I was running up the stairs. The small room I'd occupied had clothes strewn everywhere, all of the duplicates still in bags lined up against the wall. These had been fine outfits to wear here, but I didn't need the reminder of my time here haunting my closet.

I folded the shirts and pants I'd tried on and discarded in my search for something to wear and shoved them into the bags. Someone else could provide a better home for these than I could, and I doubted I could fit all this stuff in my small car anyway.

After changing into the suit I'd worn down here, I looked around the room, but nothing else belonged to me. I brushed my hands down my lapels, my suit acting like a kind of armor as I took a final snapshot of the place before I turned and headed out.

God, why did this hurt so much? This was the last thing I'd expected when I came up here, but as I walked down the hall to the stairs, the idea of saying goodbye to Micah almost seemed too much.

I stopped at the end of the hall and took in a deep breath, preparing for what I knew I had to do. Then I headed around the corner and down the stairs, where I found Micah standing in front of the fireplace.

He turned, and I crossed the small space and met him by the door.

"I almost didn't recognize you," he said, stroking my tie.

"You and me both." I tried for my best smile but knew I'd failed. "These clothes feel so tight now. So restrictive. Maybe I gained weight while I was up here?"

Micah dropped his hand and chuckled as he slipped it into his pocket. "Nah. I think you just learned to relax."

"Maybe so."

"Decide against taking anything?"

"Yeah. I figured you could donate the clothes to one of those charities you like so much."

Micah smiled softly before reaching around me to pull open the door, something I appreciated, since I felt precariously close to doing or saying something that would crack the steely barrier I was trying my hardest to erect.

I headed outside and toward the carport, and as Micah

walked beside me, I noticed Snoopy bounding alongside his leg. Huh, even the lazy mutt had come out to say goodbye—or maybe he was just here to make sure I really left.

When we reached the car I quickly unlocked it, about to make my escape, but Micah took hold of my arm and drew me into his strong embrace. I wrapped my arms around his neck and burrowed my nose in his warm skin, breathing in the woodsy pine scent that was all Micah.

My eyes stung as I fought to stave off the tears, and I couldn't stop myself from kissing him by the temple.

"I'm so happy you took the spark plugs out of my car."

Micah's deep chuckle vibrated through me as he cradled my cheek and brushed his lips over mine. "I'm so happy you have no clue about cars."

"Me too." I pulled back, swiping at my cheek, then bent down to give Snoopy a scratch on the head. "You look after him, you hear me?" When the lazy dog just yawned, I took one final look at the sexy lumberjack who'd welcomed me into his home, life, and bed, and shrugged. "I tried."

Micah grinned, and my heart did something I'd never felt it do before—it broke in half.

I gave a final nod and climbed into the car, pulling the door shut behind me, and as I went to start the engine, I'd never wished so much for it to fail. But it seemed fate had different ideas this time around, and the car purred to life.

As I backed out, I turned the car in the large space in front of the barn and waved to the man walking out to see me off.

I began to pull away, down the drive, and as I glanced in

my rearview mirror to see Micah standing just outside of the carport with his hands in his pockets and Snoopy sitting by his side, all I could think was:

I'll spend my whole life trying to get over you.

MAXWELL

Present Day

A HORN BLASTED, snapping me out of my memories. The light had turned green, but there was barely space for my car as I crossed the intersection. More honking and obscenities would come my way for sure with my ass sticking out, but I couldn't find it in me to care. Not with my mind now elsewhere.

Had it really been a year since I'd left Micah? A year since I'd spent Christmas at his tree farm with his family?

In some ways it seemed like a lifetime ago, but with the memories flooding in, it felt like yesterday. I'd driven off with him in my rearview mirror and never turned back, even though in the days and weeks that followed, I wanted to so badly. Work had taken over quickly, though; my failure at securing the Noble property had forced me to

146

find an alternative for my company. When I'd been successful in that endeavor, I was finally made a partner—something I'd been working for my whole career.

It should've made me happy. I should've felt fulfilled that I'd gone after something I wanted and done the damn thing. But the best part of it all, more than the raise, more than the new corner office, was getting a card from Micah congratulating me. How he'd found out about the job I didn't know, but it meant he hadn't forgotten me. That he still wondered how I was enough to reach out.

So of course I'd written him back thanking him, but I kept it short and sweet, not wanting to say how much hearing from him had made me miss him. I thought that would be the end of our communication, and I kept myself busy with work, keeping the long hours I was accustomed to and ordering takeout when I remembered to eat.

But every blue moon I'd get a note from him, some little reminder or picture. One was of a beautiful pond near his house in the summer that said, *It's not always snow and shovel season.* Another was a birthday card: *Sorry I didn't think to ask when you celebrate your birthday, so here's a happy birthday for the whole year.*

It always made me smile that he'd taken a minute out of his day to write me, and sometimes I wondered if they served as an invitation of sorts. Like *the door is still open, hint hint.*

Especially when the last note came a few weeks ago. It was a picture of the tree farm all lit up for their opening night, along with a note that said, *Don't forget to add a little magic to your Christmas, Scrooge.*

Was it reading too much into it to think he'd sent that

for a reason? Or maybe he was just being a nice guy and knew I was all alone in the city, stressed out as usual.

"That's a green fuckin' light, asshole!" someone yelled, and I sighed.

Add magic to my Christmas... I scoffed. How the hell was that even possible here? The answer was simple—it wasn't. As I sat there staring at the complete and utter chaos going on around me, I dreamed of that little tree farm, of the one moment in time where for a few days my life had felt...complete.

I grabbed my phone off the holder and pulled open the weather app, scrolling through until Merrihill popped up on the screen. The forecast for today was cold but clear— tomorrow, however, it looked as though an arctic blast was going to hit, with a few feet of snow expected.

I switched off the screen and tapped the side of the phone, wondering if I was really thinking what I was thinking when Nat King Cole's smooth, melodic voice came through the speakers, singing about chestnuts.

Right, that was it. I'd never been a strong believer in fate, but just like last year when Micah had stepped in to force its hand, this year I was going to do the same. There were clear signs that the universe was pointing me in a direction:

The men with the Christmas tree...

The tourists all cuddling up with each other...

The card telling me to add a little magic, and now this song —our *song.*

The only problem was, I stuck in a damn traffic jam with no way out.

It was time to take matters into my own hands.

When the light cycled through this time and turned green, I didn't care what lane I had to weave in and out of —I was moving.

I pulled the steering wheel to the left and veered into the wrong lane, and as the horns blasted all around, I wound my window down and wished them all a merry Christmas. Brakes slammed and curses were shouted as I managed to bypass the cars that had been in front of me and weave into the clearing up ahead. As I zoomed down the street in the opposite direction of my office, I reached for the volume on my car's stereo and cranked it to high, singing along to the upbeat Christmas tune that had just started.

I couldn't help the enormous smile on my face as I left the city in my rearview mirror, and as I crossed the bridge and headed out of town, it felt as though the weight of the world had been lifted off my shoulders.

I tapped the steering wheel along with the music as I glanced over at the phone sitting on my passenger seat. A niggling sense of doubt at what I was doing began to creep in, but then I thought of all those cards, of the welcoming smile Micah gave everyone who stopped by his family's farm, and I shoved it aside.

It didn't matter that I hadn't seen him in a year, *or* that I hadn't called. I was just like everyone else who was excited to come and visit the Noble Christmas tree farm.

At least, that was what I told myself the entire way there, but as I pulled onto the road that led me up to his property and saw the twinkling lights that lined his fence, that doubt turned to nerves.

I slowed the car to a crawl as I peered out at the gate

that was wide open in welcome, and lit up just as I remembered. The rows of pines were full and lush and topped with a light dusting of snow, and as I turned my car into the drive, my heart began to thump.

Already I could see the streams of people pouring through the gates, but when I saw the way they were dressed I realized it wasn't the tree farm that was open tonight, but the annual barn dance.

Oh shit. I glanced down at what I was wearing to make sure I'd fit in, but considering I'd been living in a suit for the last year, I shouldn't have been worried.

I quickly found a place to park, and once I got out of the car, I froze.

Had I really driven hours on the off chance Micah would want to see me? I hadn't given it much thought, only driven on instinct, but now that I was here... Oh God, what if he was with someone else?

No, this was stupid. I was stupid. I should just get back in my car and—

The sound of "The Christmas Song" began to filter out from the barn, and I had my answer.

Though if all these signs had pointed me in the wrong direction, I wasn't going to be a happy Scrooge.

With a stomach full of butterflies, I followed the crowd into the barn, and the wave of nostalgia that hit was so comforting it made all my nerves dissipate. There was nothing like the scent of fresh-cut trees mixed with cider, a smell I'd always associate with this place at this time of year.

The twinkling lights and garlands were strung up around the room again, and as couples began to pair off and head to the dance floor, I focused on finding the reason I was here.

Micah.

With his imposing height, he wasn't hard to find, and to my relief, he wasn't on the dance floor with someone. He stood off to the side, alone, drinking out of a paper cup as he watched the townspeople enjoying his event.

Up close and personal, he was even more handsome than I remembered. The brown locks that usually fell into his eyes were swept back tonight, and he filled out his black pants and soft crewneck sweater in a way that made my mouth water.

How was that man standing alone? It made absolutely no sense, and I moved quickly before anyone else got the bright idea to approach him.

As I stopped beside him, I tried my best to be nonchalant, but my insides felt like they were bursting. I took a deep breath and let it out slowly before saying, "Why aren't you dancing?"

Micah turned his head in my direction before the words were even out, his eyes widening and his lips parting when he saw me.

I smiled at his reaction, feeling more confident, and gave him a nudge. "I thought you liked this song."

He shook his head as a smile slowly spread across his face, and there it was: the reason I'd needed to come up here in the first place. I'd needed that smile more than I realized.

"You're here," he said, like he was trying to convince himself. "What are you doing here?"

I shrugged. "Someone told me to add a little magic to my Christmas, so I'm here to do just that."

"Oh yeah? The Noble tree farm won you over after all? I told you this place is magic."

"No." I moved in closer and reached for his hands. "You're the magic I need in my life. It's you."

Micah sucked in a breath as he stared down at me, and he didn't have to say anything—the shine of tears in his eyes told me all I needed to know.

I rubbed my thumb over his knuckles and inclined my head toward the rest of the couples. "Dance with me?"

When he nodded, I pulled him out onto the dance floor, his strong hand a familiar touch I'd missed. With Nat King Cole crooning, it was like I'd never left, but I realized then that I'd had to leave to be able to appreciate it all now.

"You're quiet tonight. Don't tell me you've forgotten how to talk while I was gone."

Micah's lips twitched as his hand tightened around my waist and he pulled me in close. "I'm still trying to work out what you're doing here, city boy."

I turned until our noses brushed. "I'm sweeping you off your feet. Can't you tell?"

Micah's eyes gleamed at the reminder of our first Christmas together. "But your job. The city. Don't you have to work tonight?"

"I do, or did, I guess. But as I sat there stuck in the middle of traffic, something much more important came up."

"More important than *your* work?"

"Mhmm." I eyed the corner of the barn where, if I

remembered correctly, a piece of mistletoe hung, and led him that way. "I remembered that I needed to kiss you."

I stopped us under the festive sprig, and Micah reached for my face. As his warm hands cradled my cheeks, every lingering bit of doubt vanished. I angled my face toward his, and at the touch of his lips, my body warmed. It was as though we'd never been apart. All of those days, weeks, and months suddenly vanished, until I was right back here where I belonged, in this winter dream.

I wrapped my arms around his neck, falling into the moment, and everything and everyone vanished from view until all I knew was Micah. It had always been Micah. The man I couldn't forget. The man I loved, the man I wanted forever.

When we finally pulled apart, Micah ran his fingers down my cheek. "You sticking around tonight, or..." His words trailed off, and I knew he was probably wondering if I was going to hightail it out of there to find the nearest five-star hotel, but I had news for him—I'd planned this all out *very* carefully.

"Actually, I was wondering if you might have a place to stay. There's a blizzard coming, you know."

Micah grinned, clearly onto my devious plan. "I did know that, but what about tomorrow and the next day?"

I sidled in close to him, wrapping my hands around his neck, and pressed a kiss to his lips. "Well, about that. You hiring?"

Micah let out a loud, joy-filled laugh and wound his arms around my waist. "For what? Couch warming? Personal shopper?"

I shoved him in the chest but couldn't help my laugh.

This was what I'd been missing. Not a thing or a place. This man.

"I don't care what you make me do, as long as at the end of the day I get to come home to you."

Micah ran his hand up my back to my neck and squeezed. "God I missed you."

I blinked back the tears welling in my eyes. His words were exactly what I'd been waiting to hear.

"I thought if I kept sending you random cards, you'd have to remember the country bumpkin you left behind."

"Ah, more like the sexy lumberjack."

"Is that right?"

"I could never forget you. I love you."

Micah rested his forehead to mine and closed his eyes. "Say that again."

I kissed my way across to his ear and whispered, "I love you, Micah Noble."

"And you want to stay? Here? With me?"

"Well, I had to get the tree farm one way or another, right?"

When Micah raised a brow, I couldn't help my burst of laughter.

"You're gonna pay for that," he said.

"Looking forward to it. And I have to say, after serious consideration, I think I'm done with acquisitions. I'm much more into couch warming these days. Or bed warming. Take your pick."

"Hmm." Micah's arms tightened around me. "The position is open, but I think I'll need to interview you first. Both on the couch and the bed. To see where you're best suited."

"If there's one thing I've learned over this past year, it's that anywhere you are is where I'm best suited."

Micah shook his head as he smiled down at me. "I can't believe such a sexy Scrooge is saying some of the sweetest things I've ever heard. You *are* Maxwell Scott, right?"

"Mhmm. But you can call me Max."

"Well just so you know, I love you too, Max. And if you want to stay, you're welcome here. Forever."

As I fell into Micah's kiss again, it felt as though my whole world had righted itself and I was exactly where, and with whom, I belonged. I was home. And forever with this man was just what I had in mind.

THANK YOU

Thank you for reading
ONCE UPON A SEXY SCROOGE.
We hope you loved Max & Micah's story as much as we
did, and that it left your heart filled with joy.

For more Ella & Brooke holiday romances you can
check out:

Wrapped Up in You
All I Want for Christmas...Is My Sister's Boyfriend
Jingle Bell Rock

***

***Love ONCE UPON A SEXY SCROOGE? Leave a review!*
Reviews are vital to authors, and all reviews, even just a couple of
quick sentences, can help a reader decide whether to pick up our
books.

*If you enjoyed this book, please consider leaving a review on the
site you purchased from.***

ALSO BY ELLA FRANK

The Exquisite Series

Exquisite

Entice

Edible

The Temptation Series

Try

Take

Trust

Tease

Tate

True

Confessions Series

Confessions: Robbie

Confessions: Julien

Confessions: Priest

Confessions: The Princess, The Prick & The Priest

Confessions: Henri

Confessions: Bailey

Prime Time Series

Inside Affair

Breaking News

Headlines

Intentions Duet

Bad Intentions

Good Intentions

Chicago Heat Duet

Wicked Heat

Wicked Flame

Sunset Cove Series

Finley

Devil's Kiss

Masters Among Monsters Series

Alasdair

Isadora

Thanos

Standalones

Blind Obsession

Veiled Innocence

Pure Seduction

PresLocke Series
Co-Authored with Brooke Blaine

Aced

Locked

Wedlocked

Fallen Angel Series

Co-Authored with Brooke Blaine

Halo

Viper

Angel

An Affair In Paris

Lust. Hate. Love

Elite Series

Co-Authored with Brooke Blaine

Danger Zone

Need For Speed

Classified

Dare To Try Series

Co-Authored with Brooke Blaine

Dare You

Dare Me

Truth Or Dare

Malvagio Series

Co-Authored with Brooke Blaine

Forbidden Mafia Prince

Sinful Mafia Prince

Standalone Novels

Co-Authored with Brooke Blaine

Sex Addict

Shiver

Secrets & Lies

Wrapped Up in You

All I Want for Christmas…Is My Sister's Boyfriend

Jingle Bell Rock

ALSO BY BROOKE BLAINE

South Haven Series

A Little Bit Like Love

A Little Bit Like Desire

The Unforgettable Duet

Forget Me Not

Remember Me When

L.A. Liaisons Series

Licked

Hooker

P.I.T.A.

Romantic Suspense

Flash Point

PresLocke Series

Co-Authored with *Ella Frank*

Aced

Locked

Wedlocked

Fallen Angel Series

Co-Authored with *Ella Frank*

Halo

Viper

Angel

An Affair In Paris

Lust. Hate. Love

Elite Series

Co-Authored with _Ella Frank_

Danger Zone

Need For Speed

Classified

Dare To Try Series

Co-Authored with _Ella Frank_

Dare You

Dare Me

Truth Or Dare

Malvagio Series

Co-Authored with _Ella Frank_

Forbidden Mafia Prince

Sinful Mafia Prince

Standalone Novels

Co-Authored with _Ella Frank_

Sex Addict

Shiver

Secrets & Lies

Wrapped Up in You

All I Want for Christmas…Is My Sister's Boyfriend

Jingle Bell Rock

ABOUT ELLA FRANK

If you'd like to get to know Ella better, you can find her getting up to all kinds of shenanigans at:

The Naughty Umbrella
(Facebook Group)

Or any of the other social media links below!

And if you would like to talk with other readers who love Ella's character's from her Chicagoverse, you can find them
HERE at
Ella Frank's Temptation Series Facebook Group.

Ella Frank is the *USA Today* Bestselling author of the Temptation series, including Try, Take, and Trust and is the co-author of the fan-favorite contemporary romance, Sex Addict. Her Exquisite series has been praised as "scorching hot!" and "enticingly sexy!"

Some of her favorite authors include Nora Roberts, Tiffany Reisz, Riley Hart, J.R. Ward, Erika Wilde, and Carly Philips.

ABOUT BROOKE BLAINE

Brooke Blaine is a USA Today Bestselling Author best known for writing romantic comedy and M/M romance. Her novels lead with humor and heart, but Brooke never shies away from throwing in something extra naughty that will scandalize her conservative Southern family for life (bless their hearts).

She's a choc-o-holic, lives for eighties bands (which means she thinks guyliner is totally underrated), believes it's always wine o'clock, and lives with the coolest cat on the planet—her Maine Coon mix, Jackson Agador Spartacus.

Brooke's Links
Brooke's Newsletter
Brooke & Ella's Naughty Umbrella

www.BrookeBlaine.com
brookeblaineauthor@gmail.com